My Demon's Name is Ed

my demon's name is Ed

DANAH KHALIL

Second Story Press

Library and Archives Canada Cataloguing in Publication

Khalil, Danah, author
My demon's name is Ed / Danah Khalil.

Issued in print and electronic formats.
ISBN 978-1-927583-96-8 (paperback).
—ISBN 978-1-77260-000-1 (epub)

I. Title.

PS8621.H334M9 2016   jC813'.6   C2016-903535-2

C2016-903536-0

Printed and bound in Canada

Second Story Press gratefully acknowledges the support of the Ontario Arts Council and the Canada Council for the Arts for our publishing program. We acknowledge the financial support of the Government of Canada through the Canada Book Fund.

Published by
SECOND STORY PRESS
20 Maud Street, Suite 401
Toronto, ON M5V 2M5
www.secondstorypress.ca

To my inspiration and mentor, Rukhsana Khan;
thank you for believing in me.

Prologue

In school we are taught about the terribly skinny people who refuse to eat, and we are told to label them *anorexic*. We are taught about the terribly skinny people who stick their fingers down their throats, and we are told to label them *bulimic*. But why aren't we taught about how they have surrendered their souls to a demon, fallen into a deep pit of solitude and misery, and contracted a disorder that inevitably changes their lives forever?

The simple response is that most educators don't understand the truth behind the disorders. All of the facts and numbers and labels we learn in the classroom don't even begin to describe the reality behind them. I am not a teacher, but I have endured, firsthand, every moment of the slow, painful descent that is an eating disorder.

I believe that, as well as balance and positivity, everyone on this earth possesses some black energy that can tear their world apart, steal their vitality, and destroy their happiness. How individuals deal with such demons varies, but be certain of this: Disguising itself behind a positive image, a disorder can find you any time it chooses to.

When I was fourteen, Ed found me almost *too* easily.

From my first encounter with the demon I call Ed to my journey down into the hole, this is my story as I recorded it.

April 3, 2012

Some call it a mental illness; one that preoccupies
your thoughts, alters your body image, and jumbles
your feelings. One that exists for a single purpose, and
wraps so tightly around you that not only does it create
misperception and denial, but also it begins to define you,
label you – become you.

Recognizing that something – or someone – has crept
inside me while I let my guard down frightens me deeply,
and it angers me to admit I am not strong enough to
fight it.

> *Do not be afraid. There is nothing to be afraid of.*
> *Do not be bitter. I am nothing to be fought.*

Am I sick? Is something wrong with me?

> *There is nothing wrong while I am in control.*

No, *yes,* no, *yes,* no, there *is* something wrong with me….
It's as if I no longer fit in my skin. Should I be concerned
by this second voice in my head, or by this second pair of
eyes on my face?

> *Stop this nonsense.*
> *Now, go drink a cup or two*
> *of water before your workout.*
> *I can hear your stomach growling.*

April 5, 2012

I look in the mirror and can't distinguish between the hazy image of Ed, the demon, desperately pleading for attention and recognition, and my own reflection that *should* be staring back at me. The demon tells me that I am too fat, that my inner thigh gap should be more noticeable, and my stomach should be flatter. It whispers in my ear – gently and soothingly, at first. Then the whispers become roars as it spits in my face. What choice do I have but to obey? I am too weak to fight; I am too afraid to try.

April 6, 2012

How to be Healthy: My Mantra

HEALTHY
Eliminate snacks.
Fewer carbs.
No eating out.
Exercise more.
Fewer calories in + more calories out = weight loss.
Exercise more.
No eating out.
Fewer carbs.
Eliminate snacks.
HEALTHY

April 7, 2012

I'm looking in the mirror after my long home workout
and feeling extremely slim and racy this morning. I finally
have defined abdominal lines. I am finally beautiful.

Just imagine how beautiful you will be twenty pounds lighter.

April 7, 2012

I'm looking in the mirror after my huge dinner and
feeling extremely chunky and bloated this evening. I
finally have reason to lose the weight. I am finally bowing
down to you, Ed.

You are all mine.

April 9, 2012

Triggers. Triggers are everywhere, pressuring me to obsess
about health, compelling me to lose weight, and insisting
that I hate myself. My dear, sweet witch of a mother,
for instance, never fails to point out my "poor eating
habits" and "lack of self-control" as I reach for yet another
spoonful of rice at the dinner table.

"Rice is a source of carbs, honey," she would warn me.
"You shouldn't eat too much of it." Well, Mother, are you
proud of my self-control now? Are you fucking satisfied
that I no longer reach for *any* rice at the table? I'll show

you self-control, Mother; just watch me eat less and less.

Another more obvious trigger, of course, is the media. In this increasingly technical generation, when it seems all we ever do is stare at screens, how can we *not* be influenced by what appears before us? As for me, I am obsessed with Tumblr. The health and fitness blogs are all so lovely, staring me right in the face, inviting me into their community. All of the bottled-up envy from watching those beautiful, athletic bodies continues to swell inside of me, pushing for more and more weight loss.

> *Must be thinner, prettier, healthier, better.*

Also, the health unit in my gym class has taught me practically everything there is to know about good nutrition and daily exercise. One might say that I have taken it slightly too far, yet my response would be that this is simply a new lifestyle – not some sort of silly, ineffective diet – and that my health has now become a priority in order to fuel my athletic performance.

For some odd reason beyond my understanding, my parents have a complete lack of trust in my new lifestyle, believing that it is not truly *healthy*.... What do they know about good health, anyway? It's clear that they feel obligated to keep an extra eye on me when they are the ones who always complained about how much I ate in the first place. It would all "catch up with me eventually," they claimed.

So why, Father, do you boom in your loud, demanding voice when I don't eat the whole hamburger? Maybe I would eat it if you didn't buy such a fatty, sodium-filled patty! We could all use some healthier choices in our diet.

My mother, on the other hand, attempts – in a somewhat caring and calm manner – to lecture me about the true definition of a "healthy body."

"I don't want to see you get any thinner," she says to me daily. "If you drop one more pound, there will be a problem."

"But why, Mom? Why will there be a problem?"

She sighs and responds, "You can't be an athlete with a skeletal structure."

I laugh in her face. Nevertheless, I see the hurt and worry in her eyes…and it scares me.

Mother does not always know best.

But what about the general public – what about everyone else telling me how much thinner I have become?

"Your legs are *so* tiny!"
"Look how small you are!"
"You sure did lose weight!"
"You have *abs!*"

"Just eat it!"
        "Are you like, anorexic?"
                "Stop counting calories!"
                        "It's just a cupcake!"

I used to feel so proud when I first began to hear
such comments, but now that I hear them so damn
frequently—

                        Oh, stop being such a baby!
                        Do not listen to them.
                        LISTEN TO ME.

But when can I begin to listen to myself?

April 10, 2012

Okay, so I am not *completely* oblivious. I do, in fact,
admit to having a few basic symptoms of eating disorders:
undereating, overexercising, counting calories, eating a
very restricted diet…and everything in between….

But I do *not* have an eating disorder! There is a huge
difference between a demon telling me how I should
eat and an eating disorder telling me not to eat *at all*,
right? And just because I prefer smaller, lighter portions
doesn't mean that I'm in trouble. Lots of girls have legs
far skinnier than mine! Plus, most people with eating
disorders binge and purge, which is something that I can
truthfully say I have never done.

We will see about that.

Okay, so perhaps I have considered it several times, but sticking a little finger down my throat would be the absolute breaking point; proof to myself that I really do have an eating disorder. I do not plan to do it, so trust me, please…~~I am totally fine!~~

Something that does frighten me, however, is that food and exercise have essentially become *all* I think about. I find it difficult to focus in school or at practice because of the constant buzz and word-vomit swirling in my mind.

"Did I overeat?"

Yes.

"Did I undereat?"

No.

"Should I do more squats?"

Yes.

"Should I stop doing push-ups?"

No.

"Am I still trying to lose weight?"

Always.

April 11, 2012

"Wow, I am so proud of your determination to live a healthy lifestyle, Danah. You're on the treadmill practically every day now!" Father praised me, as I dragged my exhausted butt past him and up the stairs after my six-mile run.

"Thanks!" I exclaimed, feeling extremely grateful that he has recognized my hard work, instead of criticizing me like Mom does every time I exercise or avoid putting any meat on my plate.

And this is only the beginning of all of the praise yet to come. Remember this feeling, and it will be yours forever.

April 12, 2012

Ed has completely changed my perspective about the upcoming school Quebec trip. Just imagining all the crap I will be forced to eat and knowing that my workouts will be limited knots my stomach, causes my palms to sweat and my head to spin. Let me guess. This is *not* normal. Surely no one else worries about such mundane things to this extent. Should I be concerned? The absolute most my friends will ever worry about regarding the trip is if their tongues are far enough down their boyfriends' throats, or if they are wearing enough makeup…. Fucking pathetic.

Nevertheless, I have a master plan: nibble at the

restaurants, skip lunch, don't eat snacks, and exercise every
night in the hotel room.

Shit.
That can't be a good plan.
So why did I just write it down?
Why am I unable to adjust it?

> *You don't want to see all of our progress*
> *go down the drain in four short days, do you?*

How will I carry out my plan without everyone eyeballing
me? I can just imagine their snide comments and stares
now. I'm quite certain I will gain the *bulimic* label to add
to the *anorexic* one.

Why must this all be so stressful?

Anger boils deep inside me. I want to shout in their faces:

> "HOW DOES MY LACK OF
> EATING AFFECT YOU? STICK
> YOUR TONGUES BACK
> DOWN YOUR BOYFRIENDS'
> THROATS, AND I SHALL STICK
> MY FINGER DOWN MINE.
> YES, I'M WORKING OUT
> RIGHT NOW BECAUSE,
> UNLIKE YOU HIGH-
> METABOLISM *STICKS*, I WILL
> GAIN WEIGHT IF I DON'T.

AND I *DO NOT* WANT TO
GAIN WEIGHT.
AND NO, GODDAMN IT,
I WILL NOT EAT THE
DESSERT. I WON'T TASTE IT,
SNIFF IT, OR EVEN LOOK AT
IT. YOU WILL NEVER MAKE
ME…. YOU WILL NEVER
UNDERSTAND."

Jesus, so just don't go!

Don't go?

Stay home; stay under my watch.

Stay home?

Stay within my comfort and care.

Comfort and care?

But haven't I already paid?
What will my excuse be?
What will my friends say?

Am   I   really   considering
            this   right   now?

A part of me actually recognizes that Quebec might even be a good, healthy experience for me – shockingly enough.

Oh, please.

Maybe, just maybe, it will teach me that it is totally acceptable to treat myself once in a while. ... So, why am I struggling to believe myself? Am I too damn pessimistic and stubborn to allow a tiny bit of light to shine through and warm my dark thoughts?

April 16, 2012

It's raining way too hard to go on my hourly walk with the dog. If it were up to me, I would suit up as though it was completely sunny outside, but my parents wouldn't let me.

Even after I begged.
And cried.
And angrily stormed out of the room.

I *have* to go for my walk.

It is not an option.
It is not an option.
It is not an option.

I ate far too big of a piece of salmon – *super* high in fat – for dinner, which means I cannot afford to skip this walk.

Now, Mom and Dad are so pissed with me for having

a temper tantrum that they will not even drive me to the gym as promised. There is probably no way they would drive me to the gym, anyway. Not in this weather. Fucking wussies. It's just a bit of rain.

What do I do?
Ed is going to kill me.

Maybe I will go for a walk in the basement.
But what if my parents see me?
Fuck it.
I need to walk.
I ate too much salmon.

April 17, 2012

I'm worried that someone will read these entries and think I am an absolute nutcase – maybe even bipolar – and so I will try to describe my constant, inner turmoil as accurately and realistically as possible.

Imagine two cartoon characters – one angel and one devil – appear on either shoulder and begin to bicker. They do not stop bickering, arguing so loudly that my head feels as though it might very well split right down the center. It always ends the same way; the cold, harsh devil beats the mild, long-suffering angel. The devil *always* wins, as he reduces any positive thoughts to dust and tosses it over his shoulder.

But this is not a cartoon. This is real. The demon has

taken over…. Acceptance is the first step to recovery, no?

Recovery!?
Baby, you are perfectly fine.

No. No I am *not* – I am like a fucking mental illness
patient!

Calm down.
Don't ever raise your voice to me.

April 19, 2012

"Danah, everything in moderation. Please, have a tiny
piece of cake. Look. Your sister and I are eating it," Mother
said soothingly as she took a bite of that warm, chocolate
lava cake. "You see? Nothing bad will happen to us."

Fuck.
My mouth is salivating.
Do it.
Take a bite.
Just one bite.
What?

Do not do it.
Don't you dare take a bite!
Just because they do it doesn't mean you have to.
They are not as fit and healthy as you.
They don't give a damn about you.
They want to see you get fat.

But it looks so good…. And after all, I did just step off the treadmill after an hour's run. The treadmill says I burned over 500 calories, which is probably as much as the portion of the cake. It will be as though I didn't even eat it….

I think I am going to do it.
My mom and sister are staring at me.
I have to do it.

It tastes so fucking delicious.
It's warm and soft and moist and indulgent.
My stomach is smiling.
It is the best thing I have ever eaten in my entire life.

*Good, because it will be the last
thing for a long, long time.*

Fuck.
What have I done?
Am I fucking crazy?
Why would I do that?
I fucking hate my mom and sister for making me do that.
If they want to get fat they can LEAVE ME OUT OF IT!
Fucking morons.
No, I can't blame them.
It's my fault for having no self-control.
The only fucking moron here is me.
Now I have to go work it off.
If I am lucky, I will "get sick" and puke.

April 20, 2012

Height: 5'5"
Initial weight: 125 pounds.
Current weight: 105 pounds.

One side of me is jumping with glee.
The other has already admitted defeat.

It is just too late.
I took a deep plunge into rock bottom.

April 26, 2012

Ed welcomes me home this evening after I barely
managed to survive the Quebec trip, all thanks to my
masterful plan of skipping lunches and – despite the dire
warnings and comments from my peers – doing a full-
body workout every night. My intense fear of gaining
weight added so much pressure to the trip, however,
that it was nearly impossible to enjoy any of it; not one,
small moment. Having to refuse all of those scrumptious
desserts and having to ignore my stomach as it called out
for food at lunchtimes was quite a miserable experience.

But that was a proper display of self-control.
And now, you have mastered it.

Should I be proud of my newly acquired self-control,
or should I be frightened of it?

The trip certainly didn't help my case for ditching the *anorexic* label. In fact, it made the situation far, far worse.

Who cares what others think?
Ignore them all.
Listen to me.
Only me.

On the third day, during lunch, my friends approached me in a considerably caring manner, as I awkwardly watched them all dive into their *poutine*. I do understand that they were only trying to look out for me, but no one can fathom that I am not seeking help. Why does everyone assume that I am? I know very well what I am doing and I can take care of myself just fine.

Can I, though? Can I really look after myself? The problem has now become too mentally and physically challenging to overcome; I truly do not see myself ever taking that first, hefty step toward "recovery".

Despite all of the crazy, mixed emotions and ideas running through my mind, the one thing I know for certain is that I do *not* want to see that I have lost weight as I step on the scale tomorrow.

Really?

Yes, because I realize that would be a terrible sign.

You are kidding, right?

> *You starved yourself for four days*
> *and you don't want to see positive results?*

But why must *more* weight loss be the only answer, the only positive result? What's so wrong with maintaining my current weight?

> *Maintenance is for losers with no self-control.*

Shit.
Guess who will not be getting any sleep tonight.
I will be too busy dancing with Ed in my nightmares.
Nightmares. Nightmares.
Good night.
Don't let the demons bite.

April 27, 2012

100 pounds.

NO!

> *Yes!*

NO!

> *Yes!*
> *Shut up and be proud.*
> *It's better than gaining weight, fat-ass.*

April 28, 2012

I have become the regular topic of everyone's conversations. *Everyone's.* Whether I'm at school, at home, or at soccer, I am constantly judged and gossiped about. And the result is quite simple: the more everyone continues to talk, the less I listen. The pressure it adds to my narrow shoulders and terrified soul only makes matters far, *far* worse.

The guidance counselor, teachers, parents, friends – they all worry. Why must everyone worry about me?

Worry.
      Worry.
            Worry.

WHY DON'T
THEY JUST MIND
THEIR OWN
BUSINESS AND
WORRY ABOUT
THEMSELVES?

They cannot possibly understand my situation, anyhow. I am playing a completely different game than they are.

So, what is the point?
What is the point of my family
lecturing me about my new diet?

What is the point of seeking a dietitian,
a nutritionist, or some professional?
What is the point of everyone pushing
me in the "right" direction?
What is the point of discussing my "issues"
in the guidance office?
There is no point.

April 29, 2012

I never took this journey down the trail of transformation, intending to wander so far that I couldn't turn back. Nor did I ever intend to affect the lives of loved ones with my collapse. I didn't mean to make them worry as much as they do. This combat is no longer just between the demon and me.

My metamorphosis is expected to end where it all began: inside of me. Inside of my seething brain. To retrace my steps, to fall back into old routines, to go back in time, to stop myself from falling into the demon's first trap…I must destroy the new me. I must break free of the demon's grasp. I must climb until I escape from the dark, lonesome pit. I must avoid Ed's hungry eyes. I must ignore his shouting – place my hands over my ears, shut my eyes, hug my knees, suck my thumb, and rock and cry until this miserable nightmare ends. That is all this truly is; one B I G, terrifying nightmare.

April 30, 2012

Up to now my mother has never uttered such powerful, cruel words to my face. Of course, my immediate response was to cry and to wallow in denial.

The words slid off her tongue much too easily.

"You   have   an   eating   disorder."

Sticks and stones…
Your mother is a bitch, anyway.

May 1, 2012

My first appointment with a dietitian is scheduled for this Wednesday, and I am far too numb for the severity of the situation to sink in. Writing it down, hearing the words… it has become totally meaningless to me; it simply slips right by.

But I do wonder. Will I be forced to do as she says?

YOU ONLY TAKE ORDERS FROM ME.

But she is a professional.

BUT I AM FAMILY.

Okay,
    okay,
        okay,
            okay….

But I should at least take what she says into consideration.
Baby steps only, I promise.

                        I will tear this dietitian bitch apart.
                      No one dares to step between you and me.

Fine,
    fine,
        fine,
            fine….

I won't agree to gain weight, but I *do* want to stop these
conflicting thoughts of mine.

      Deep down, you know that I am not going anywhere.

May 2, 2012

"It is not about the weight, and certainly it isn't about
the calories. It's about prioritizing and repairing your
emotional and physical health." —Dietitian

            I promise *(not)* to replace my three
     daily fruit snacks with higher-content options.

I promise *(not)* to consume richer grades of
milk, yogurt, cheese, and cereal.

I promise *(not)* to add an additional snack
upon arriving home from school.

I *(do not)* understand that
athletes require starch for energy.

I *(do not)* understand that the weight
I gain will be favorable fat and muscle.

I *(do not)* understand that I will appear
much healthier having gained some weight.

Regardless of the situation, gaining weight is immensely
discouraging and unpleasant, whether it is necessary or
not. The suggested changes are tough pills to swallow, for
the truth is stuck in my throat, refusing to go down. I
guess this was all bound to happen eventually. I just didn't
expect it to be this difficult to accept.

Somebody please, *please,* put me out of my misery.

May 5, 2012

Once strong, toned, and aggressive; my athletic build has
fallen behind me.

Now weak, scrawny, and frail;
my confidence has vanished from within me.
No longer beautiful, radiant, and energetic;
my aura has decayed within me.
I still dream of being healthy, muscular, and fit.
But in order to accomplish this ideal image…
must I truly gain weight?

May 6, 2012

Mother, Mother

Your lips quiver; they cause your words to shake.
Your nails are raw, bitten right down to the nub.
Your hair is graying; it twists and twirls through your
nervous fingers.
Your eyes fidget, avoiding my pleading gaze.
Your voice is hushed; it exposes your fear.

But trust me, Mother, no one is as afraid as I.

You guilt my soul until it crumbles.
You pull the strings of my heart until they snap.
You beg and beseech until my ears shatter.
You pressure my disorder until I cave in.

You fight the demon so it will surrender.

But trust me, Mother, the demon does not lose.

May 9, 2012

The calories were delectable,
spreading comforting warmth down my throat…
Like Smirnoff and Grey Goose.

The calories were painful,
spreading cruel apathy through your heart…
Like arrows and knives.

May 13, 2012

I   have   an   eating   disorder
and   I   need   help.

No more denying, no more hiding. The ink has been applied to this page permanently; the words have been released from my lips into the air for all time. Admitting the cold, distasteful truth is, inevitably, the first step to my recovery.

But you do not want to recover.

May 19, 2012

I was moisturizing my legs today after exiting the shower and could not help but notice how strong, tight, and muscular my calves felt. It must be because of all of the calf raises I have been doing before bed.

May 20, 2012

"Eat more + exercise less = weight gain."

The answer should be crystal clear with everyone shouting these words in my face. So why do conflict and doubt haunt me and compel me to run in the opposite direction?

Run faster.
Farther.
Do not stop.

May 24, 2012

The most difficult pill of all to swallow during this quest for recovery is the knowledge that I was *finally* fucking satisfied with my body. So I ask myself, why should I tear apart all of my fortified self-esteem? Why must I undo my hard-won self-control?

May 25, 2012

"I'll get it!" I exclaimed, as the ball scooted behind the net and down the path once more. For about the tenth time I sprinted to retrieve it, and brought it back at breakneck speed. "I gotta work off that slice of pizza I ate last night," I said, panting, as my teammates exchanged furtive glances.

"Yeah, okay. You know that is probably only burning off, like, *one bite,* right?" one of my friends snorted.

Fuck. She was right. Why isn't practice more physically demanding? Far too much time is spent talking and just standing around.

SOMEONE BRING ON THE FITNESS PLEASE!
I HAVE FAT I NEED TO BURN OFF!!
WHERE ARE THE LADDERS?
THE HURDLES??
THE CONES???
PLEASE!!!!

May 30, 2012

Despite the dietitian's orders, the doctor's warnings, and my family's pleas, I still find myself secretly wishing to remain the same.

SO STAY THE SAME!

But it is *so* difficult to ultimately love myself when discouraging words are constantly spat in my face:

"Unhealthy,

Underweight,

Unnourished,

Unhealthy,

Unhealthy

Unhealthy,

Unhealthy."

They force bigger portions down my throat. They badger me again and again.

Can't they see that I am trying?

But are you, really?

May 31, 2012

Daily Intake:

Breakfast
1 cup shredded wheat cereal
1 miniature 0% fat fruit yogurt
1 cup skim milk
1 banana
1 water bottle

Morning Snack
1 apple
100-calorie packaged cookie
1 water bottle

Lunch
2 slices whole wheat bread
1 slice low fat cheese
1 piece romaine lettuce
1 water bottle

Afternoon Snack
1 orange
100-calorie packaged cookie
1 water bottle

Dinner
* TINY PORTION OF DAD'S DISH ALONG WITH
1 WATER BOTTLE
* CARB-FREE MEAL IF POSSIBLE

* NO EVENING SNACK – DRINK WATER IF
HUNGRY

Daily Sweat:

Home Workout
30 squats
30 calf raises
30 push-ups
30 crunches
30 sit-ups
30 weighted back row push-ups
30 weighted bicep curls
30 weighted single triceps extensions
30 weighted knee to elbow crunches
30 weighted cross-punches
1-minute plank
1-minute 6-inch feet lift
30 sun salutations
10-minute stretch

Cardio
1 hour walk with dog * PUMPING ARMS; FAST PACE
Soccer practice/game OR 30-minute treadmill run

June 6, 2012

Life has been treating me very unkindly, lately…. I
suppose life is much tougher for many other people out
there, but I am still practically just a child! People my
age should only be concerned about boys, school, and
friendships; not demons, disorders, and dark holes.

To genuinely accept change and commit to it is exceptionally challenging. Thankfully, I have persuaded myself to begin making slight adjustments to my diet and restrict my daily exercise to a smaller chunk of time, but I am still struggling with the addition of larger snacks and the idea of eating "junk food." The disorder is forcing me to stay within its boundaries, and unfortunately, junk food is way beyond its barbed-wire fencing.

I repeatedly question my mother's tactics. How can she expect me to obsess *less* about my eating habits and my body while all of her endless bullshit forces me to stress even *more* about it every damn day?

To make matters worse, she and the doctor had the marvelous idea of enrolling me in a "special program" at the hospital where I will be surrounded by other fucked up, far-too-skinny teen girls. I'm not certain when this will begin, but the moment it does, I will officially be branded as an "eating disorder patient."

June 9, 2012

I am not ready I am not ready I am not ready.

I am not ready to fully commit to the idea of gaining weight.

Neither am I.

It appears as though everyone expects it to come so effortlessly. Surely they must be thinking *Why hasn't she just gained weight already? It's so easy!* Ha! It's obviously much easier for someone who does *not* have an eating disorder. How is it that no one is able to grasp the concept of keeping weight off?

As opposed to taking the "easy way out" – eating more, working out less – I remain almost exactly the same as before; I am unable to break my habits. I'm still obsessive and obligated to plan out my daily meals, and the idea of food, on the whole, still utterly terrifies me. I refuse to consume any food not on my daily meal plan, no matter how badly I crave it. My self-control is so powerful that I don't even need to think twice about it anymore.

June 10, 2012

Exams are approaching, but I am finding it increasingly difficult to prepare because the only two subjects that ever seem to cross my mind are food and exercise. My grades really have dropped this year, and it is *not* because of the greater workload or the more challenging material. It's because Ed has forced me to become undisciplined in my studies.

> *Well, duh.*
> *School is a waste of your time.*
> *Imagine how much skinnier you'd be*
> *if you weren't cooped up in a classroom all day.*
> *Besides, the only education you will*
> *ever need from now on is from me.*

June 12, 2012

Just a couple of hours ago, I was pressing my ear to
Mother's bedroom door, listening to the most excruciating
of conversations. She has now formally admitted me into
the clinic program at the hospital,

and
I
feel
like
dying.

I am certainly not in a position to commit suicide at this
time. But the mere idea of it – stubbornly nestled in the
back of my mind, practically begging to be released – has
tempted me on numerous occasions to give it serious
thought. I have been trying my hardest not to pour that
dark, dreaded thought onto these pages, but in the wake
of my enrollment, I knew that it was time. Although I am
not certain of when, I know that the sessions – and the
torture – will soon begin. I have already been warned on
several occasions that if I do not gain weight, I will be fed
through tubes.

NOBODY UNDERSTANDS WHERE I AM
COMING FROM!!! It is not *my* fault that my mind
restricts weight gain and additional intake. People with
eating disorders are panicky about overeating and are,
essentially, controlled by a second personality. How can I

possibly be expected to gain weight when I have a demon constantly running its mouth off in my head? My fears of food never fail to stand like strong, tall barriers to my recovery.

June 13, 2012

I restrict and I refrain and I retreat and I run. Mom bitches and cries and pleads and yells, thus creating a monstrous cycle of negativity and reluctance. She is always right up my ass and always right under my nose. Right now, more than anything, I just want to be left ALONE. No family, no friends, no demon. Will I ever get back to normal? Can I return to the moment just before Ed took complete control; back to when I could eat and exercise without fuss, without planning, without calculations? It is far too late for that, isn't it? Ed – the demon – has crept inside of me, opened wide, and swallowed me whole. Recovery seems virtually impossible. Shouldn't I just give up—

> *Get real, honey.*
> *You were never really trying.*

Or should I fight my way through the unhealthy thoughts? It is too challenging to decide, when all I can see is darkness inside the hole.

> Me against the disorder…
> Me against the demon…
> Me against myself.

June 14, 2012

Current weight: 97.89 pounds.

Goal accomplished!

I   cannot   be   saved.

June 15, 2012

Nobody will ever truly be able to figure out why I continue to avoid help and the outstretched arms of my friends and family. I can barely comprehend any of my own actions or thoughts myself. Can anyone out there patch me up or break through my tough shell? Will anyone be able to read these lines and discover the true cause of it all? How do I explain to people that some sort of demon lurking in my mind is what controls me? Will I ever be able to escape from this new, scary me?

As I continue to stumble farther and farther into the darkness, deeper and deeper into the murky water, and lower and lower into the familiar pit, I know that I will never be strong enough to come up for air and fill my lungs with sweet, calming wind – nourish my mind with positivity and clarity. I will never be strong enough to break free from the grasp of the demon that is pulling me down.

This dangerous, dark spirit has simply wrenched my world

a p a r t.

June 19, 2012 (14th Birthday)

I wonder if…

Ed has already taken over.
I will become fat and unfit from all of the food
and lack of exercise.
The pain will prove too much for me.
I will ever discover the answers I need to
help heal my body and mind.
My mother is disappointed in me.
I will ever be allowed to run again.
I will have to spend the nights away from
home at the hospital.
My self-confidence will be shattered
from the weight gain.
I am causing the stress and worry of others.
The demon is always right.
I will remain a strong athlete.
My father is scared and confused.
I will ever be healthy again.
The therapists at the hospital will understand.
I will learn to have a balanced diet.
I am overthinking everything.
I will be forced to drop all forms of exercise.

I can trust my friends enough to ask for their help.
I will overcome my fear of food and weight gain.
I will eventually break all of my new habits.
There will be at least one moment to enjoy this summer.
I will cry more than I will smile.
My body image is distorted.
I am too bony.
I will be yanked deeper into the hole.
My friends will talk behind my back.
I will be monitored 24/7.
I have lost all authority over myself.
I will be weighed daily.
My mother cries herself to sleep because of me.
I will spend one day without the
worries or stress of my eating disorder.
I will become even more depressed and anti-social.
My mother feels guilty for ruining my summer.
I will be able to be a regular kid again.
Everyone is exaggerating.
I will ever be fast enough to run away from the demon.
This journey will become increasingly difficult.
I will have to stay in the
hospital program for a long, long time.
I will get my period back.
I am still losing weight.
I will have to quit soccer.
My life will ever get back to normal.
I will purge for the first time.
I will ever escape from the hole.
I can eventually find balance between diet
and exercise.

Suicidal thoughts will cross my mind again.
I will ever find recovery.
Anyone can save me from myself.

June 20, 2012

I was feeling quite nostalgic on my birthday yesterday,
so I decided to flip open an old childhood photo album
of mine…. Little did I know that I would be absolutely
appalled – and frankly repulsed – by its contents.

I really was the fattest baby I had ever fucking laid my
eyes on. Suddenly, the rolls on my arms and legs and the
chubbiness of my cheeks that I once found so adorable
were now frightening me; making me worry that any baby
who grew up with such a round, overweight body must be
destined to have a slow metabolism for the rest of its life.
Jesus, now I really am fucked. Why did my damn parents
have to have such a fat fucking kid, anyway? My sister was
never that large.

Do not worry, baby, you still win.
You are far smaller than she is now.

June 22, 2012

Skeletor.
Skeletor.
Skeletor.
Skeletor.
Skeletor.
Skeletor.
Skeletor.
Skeletor.

Skeletor.
Skeletor.
Skeletor.
Skeletor.

Skeletor.
Skeletor.
Skeletor.
Skeletor.

Skeletor.
Skeletor.
Skeletor.
Skeletor.

The word rang in my head, over and over and over again, until tears finally began to pour out of me. My friend quickly spun me around so that my back was facing the rest of the team. She took me far away from everyone.

"I know, I know. I'm sorry," she replied comfortingly. "But honestly, fuck him. He is a dick. He is an insensitive, oblivious, heartless dick. Seriously."

I continued to blubber until finally, words managed to escape my lips. "God, I am just so *angry* – even more so than hurt…. Like, I thought he was my friend. Friends don't go around calling each other *Skeletor*. He *knows* I have a serious problem!"

"So you know what you have to do tonight? You have to channel all of that anger and just play your heart out. Every time you go in for a tackle, pretend the ball or the other player is his big, stupid head."

I couldn't help but smile, as I brought my friend in for a long hug, before we both returned to the warm-up.

I wish I could have made my friend – and myself – proud tonight by going out there and playing my hardest like I promised, but I didn't. I played for five minutes, and then I crawled behind the bench to stretch for the rest of the game like the pathetic loser I am.

June 25, 2012

"Danah, we need to talk about something," one of my closest friends says, as we walk around the field at lunch. The fucking second the words cross her lips, I know *exactly* what this talk is going to be about. Still, I ask anyway.

"Is it bad or good?"

"Uh," she replies with an awkward chuckle, "let's go with bad."

She opens a piece of paper that has been folded small, as if it were a top-secret mission or something. This only confirms my suspicion that the talk will certainly be about my eating disorder.

"So, you know, my mom really cares about you, and she really just wants to see you get better and eat. So she would really appreciate you taking a look at this letter she wrote for you."

Hesitantly, I take the hand-written letter from her and shove it in my pocket, before mumbling, "Thanks."

This girl has some fucking nerve, eh? Her *and* her damn mother! Okay, sure, it is extremely thoughtful and all of her to write this letter to me, but does she *really* think her bullshit advice will help? All she did was emphasize what

I already know: I need to eat or else I will be put into a hospital.

Well, NEWS FLASH, LADY: I already *am* admitted to the hospital, so I guess you are just too fucking late.

June 29, 2012

Please help I ate a deep-fried taco downtown I did not know that it would be deep-fried and I need help I feel so fat and bloated it had cheese and beans and tofu and I did not know it would be deep-fried please Ed don't be mad I didn't know I did *not* know but now I have to go to the gym even though I already did my home workout this morning but I wonder if that will be too much exercise please help I do not know what to do but I know I hate feeling this fat and tomorrow I will barely eat anything at all.

July 2, 2012

My first trip to the 8th floor of the hospital left me suffering, with no choice but to suck it up and to start *trying* – trying to gain weight, trying to increase my heart rate, trying to achieve true health, trying to cleanse my tainted mind, and trying to recover.

My heart rate was so dangerously low that they threatened to lock me up in the hospital that night, but after countless tears – mine and my mother's – were spilled, I was granted another chance.... I have been given just one week to improve my weight and heart rate; otherwise I will be admitted to the overnight program. The very thought of that sends shivers down my spine and concerns buzzing through my mind. What if I'm not allowed to do my daily abdominal exercises and have to be fed through tubes!? It's all so damn horrifying.

Of course, "eating more" isn't the only requirement. I am now forced to cut nearly all exercise from my life, including my hourly walks with the dog and my home workouts. One thing that I refused to sacrifice was soccer. Not because I am incredibly passionate or talented or anything like that, but because I know that my sudden absence in the middle of the season would cause everyone – parents, teammates, and coaches – to come to their own conclusions…. The drama and the bullshit would never end.

Despite my promise to really begin to try, I have secretly been disobeying their orders behind everyone's backs.

That's my girl!
You sneaky thing….

Yes, every day I continue to do my quick workouts, especially on days with no physical activity. That should be allowed anyway, shouldn't it? I am an athlete; they can't take away all of my exercise! I have to stay fit and toned. I must have a six-pack. I must work hard daily.

Good girl.

My second appointment tomorrow will determine if overnight hospitalization is mandatory. I don't believe I have ever been so terrified and anxious in my entire life. It is hard to say whether or not I have gained weight because my mother has hidden her bathroom scale. My body image and perception of myself are just so fucked that looking in a mirror tells me absolutely nothing. I only see through the eyes of the demon. And he sees my entire body with fat needing to be lost.

Despite all the extra food that I consumed this week – three granola bars, Boost, and fairly large meal portions – could I somehow have *lost* weight?

That would be excellent!

The third option, of course, is that I have *maintained* my weight. I wonder what result that would have: hospitalization and punishment, or encouraging words and greater freedom?

July 3, 2012

I felt an overwhelming amount of anxiety and anticipation as I entered the elevator and walked down the 8th floor hallway. My heart was beating faster than a hummingbird's wings, and my palms were wet with perspiration. Dizziness made my head spin so that I could barely read the EATING DISORDERS sign above me. It was as if I were dyslexic.

After a urine test and many shaky prayers, I stepped onto the scale. When I finally opened my eyes to see what my fate would be, absolute relief washed over me.

I
Gained
Five
Whole
Pounds.

Seeing the number 102 on the scale released such an astounding amount of emotion that I bawled like a baby, crying from relief and happiness.

No, you cried from sadness and fear.
You cried because you knew that I would punish you severely.

Despite my tears of joy, fear hit me hard as my mind snapped back to reality. Conflicting emotions and questions resumed their race to the finish line in my head. My biggest concern of all: how much farther must I go? How much more weight do I have to gain before I am considered healthy? I know that the doctors don't want to give me a specific number of pounds, but I *must* know what their magic number is…. Will it be when my period returns? Or when my heart rate increases substantially? Or will it be when I simply appear healthier? What exactly is needed for me to achieve recovery? I do not want to be back where I was before – at 125 pounds with poor eating habits – so maybe just a few more pounds will do ~~and everything will be okay again.~~

Nothing over 105, that's for sure.

Unfortunately, the final magic number is not up to me to decide.

You are quite right. It's up to me.

Judging from the ridiculous amount of Boost that my mother has recently bought, it looks as though she thinks I need a weight goal of more than 125....

But—
But—
But that's FAT!
YOU WILL BE FAT.
FAT.
FAT.

I am honestly not certain I will be able to keep up this weight gain for another week. I am so deeply trapped within the pit, connected to a demon who refuses to loosen his tight grip on me. Separation from my eating disorder is the key to becoming myself again, but both separation and recovery appear to be out of my reach at this point. Despite the small weight gain and shaky step up the first rung of the ladder, I find myself still staring into the darkness and into the piercing eyes of my demon. How will I ever attain complete separation from the voice that has taken complete control of my entire being – mind, body, and soul? The disorder still occupies its reserved seat inside of me. It continues to override my thoughts and actions.

I want it GONE – the pressures, the worries, the fears, the conflicting voices, the mixed emotions – I want it *all* gone.

July 10, 2012

I wish I could ~~go biking~~ *do bicycle crunches.*
I wish I could ~~go running~~ *do runners' lunges.*
I wish I could ~~go swimming~~ *do swimmers' pushups.*

I miss my friends.

I am the only friend you need.

I miss fun.

We have fun together.

I miss summer.

Enjoy the view from your bedroom window.

July 15, 2012

There was absolutely nothing interesting on television as I was secretly running on the treadmill this afternoon. I settled for a kids' channel and watched cartoons, and for the first time in a long time while exercising, I actually felt genuinely happy as the bittersweet nostalgia hit home.

I even managed to crack a smile.

July 16, 2012

More tears were shed and more negative voices were heard at today's hospital appointment. Despite last week's incredible five-pound weight gain, my insecurities started to percolate and create doubt while waiting for my results. Certainly, I kept up with the same eating habits as the week before, yet my disorder kept challenging me, causing more worry to creep in.

Nonetheless, I was pleasantly surprised by the numbers that appeared on the little, square screen as I stepped on the scale once more. Another five-pound increase! I should feel ecstatic, but the voice in my head doing battle with that of my nurse confirmed that I am not even *relatively* close to being finished just yet. When I asked the question that had been occupying my mind all week – How much more weight must I gain? – her response was "Until you look and feel healthy. Your period is a sign of your body's health. You need that period back."

I tried to explain to her that my period, even before the weight loss, was always quite irregular due to my athleticism and active lifestyle. Still, she insisted that although it might take a while, my period would come back once I reached a normal, healthy weight.

On the downside of today's appointment, my therapist suggested my family participate with me in a joint therapy program once a week. I completely lost it upon hearing this. I have already gained *ten* pounds all by myself, and this is my fucking reward? Obviously, I am capable of continuing this progress by myself; I do *not* need the rest of my family sticking their noses even farther up my ass…. I don't want to drag them down with me…. I do not want them to catch even a glimpse of my messed-up mind.

July 19, 2012

I have attempted to explain to my therapist the root of my downfall countless times, but I feel as though she doesn't trust that I am telling the whole truth.

> *Perhaps this is because you are not.*

Well, how do I explain to her that on my quest for healthier eating habits and self-control, a demon has wiggled inside of my mind, shoved me into a pit, and caused a disorder that determines my every step?

I realize that I have made a grave mistake, but I have faith that I will fix it.

> *No, you will not.*

I actually almost believe myself when I say that I am able to fix this; the ball is in my court. I *will* regain the healthy weight from eating good fats, protein, and clean carbs. I *will* become toned and remain fit. I *will* maintain my newly developed self-control and healthy eating habits while feeling happy and pure. I will *not* suffer from the inner turmoil that the demon thrusts my way. For once – despite Ed doubting me constantly – I feel lighter… mentally, of course, since I am physically heavier.

Heavier and fattier and uglier.

July 24, 2012

Well, Ed must be feeling utterly overjoyed from the result of today's appointment. I sure hope he's fucking satisfied.

Precisely.

I should not have expected progress at the same rate weekly. Still, I was shocked to see the numbers actually *fall* three pounds to 104! Overwhelmed by confusion, fear, and frustration, I burst into tears. Concern and doubt flooded my mind with the force of a waterfall. Would they put me into the overnight program, despite my advances of the previous weeks? Would they tell my mother? As though I were a little child who had just been sent to the principal's office, I had butterflies fluttering in my stomach.

Or was that just the growling from your lack of breakfast this morning?

Despite my mental disruption in the wake of the news, I was awfully surprised to find that both my doctor and my mother took a gentle approach in reassuring me that I am strong enough not only to gain those three measly pounds back, but to also gain more.

After all, with my body and metabolism beginning to make adjustments to all of the extra food I've been eating, it's perfectly normal for my weight to fluctuate in the process, right?

You see?
I told you, it is normal to lose weight.
You must keep going.
Keep going.

Keep going? But, what if I lose more weight next week? How do I play this game – is it three strikes and I'm out?

Sometimes, it is so hard to believe in recovery. I may be gaining weight now, but what will happen in a couple of months, or in a couple of years, once I have exited the hospital program? Will Ed still be here? Will the hole trap me again? Will I ever truly heal from the disorder's destruction?

On another sour note, I agreed to the family therapy program in an attempt to prove to my therapist that I truly desire a healthy change to occur within me. Perhaps it will not be as agonizing and useless as I suspect.

July 26, 2012

It is a great comfort to me, knowing that I am strong enough to stare at practically any food and simply walk away – even as my stomach growls from starvation and my body aches from malnourishment.

Food, at the moment, feels to me like the only aspect of my life over which I have complete control. I *crave* self-control; greater self-control equals less consumption. But stretching that self-control too far is what caused the stranger's voice in my mind and the foreign figure under my skin to emerge victorious. I may have learned to control my appetite, but I cannot control myself from dancing with the disorder. I may have become strong enough to exercise for hours a day, but I cannot gather the strength to climb out of the pit.

July 31, 2012

Last week's drop has been erased as though it had never happened. My weight has climbed back up to 107 pounds, and although a smile may have crossed my lips, tears began to fall later, during the first family therapy session. How is it that can I be so physically strong, yet so emotionally weak? Seeing my mother tear up as well triggered more non-stop crying. I couldn't help it. I feel so undeniably guilty for all of the pain and worry I have caused her. Why must she cry? She needs to be strong for us both.

Strangely enough, I don't mind my therapist. She doesn't mention weight or calories very often, since, as she explains, the main goal is for me to achieve separation from my disorder. But I have yet to close the vast distance between recovery and me, for the demon sticks to me like Super Glue.

We are inseparable.
Forever melded into one.

It is quite challenging to open up to my therapist one-on-one, but with my parents present, it is even more problematic. One day, I hope to be able to tell them the entire truth. Perhaps until I describe every harrowing detail aloud, I will never truly heal.... But right now, I'm too busy holding back tears to speak, and the demon's ghastly hand over my mouth is forbidding me to tell the truth.

Lately, I have had to eat even *more* than usual to compensate for my secret workouts at home; volleyball practice sessions in the backyard, and soccer three times a week. I have to tell myself repeatedly that eating more to balance my exercise routine is both crucial and normal to avoid a mental breakdown. I love to enhance my fitness, and I love to eat, so essentially, it is a win-win....

But is it though? With Ed still breathing down my neck and whispering in my ear, I believe everything he tells me:

Keep doing crunches,
and then you can have one extra meatball.

August 1, 2012

In three days, my family and I (unfortunately) must leave for another (terrible) fucking family vacation. This year, we are venturing to the "magical" city of New York, but our trips are always far from relaxing and cheerful.

Although I anticipate this vacation to have its usual share of bickering and bitching, I have no doubt that it will go down on record as one of the most chaotic in family history because of the extra guest in our hotel room, Ed. I feel as though I am tearing my family apart. My mother cries, my dad roars, and my sister fusses that no one is paying any attention to her. Certainly, all eyes will be locked on me this week; noting what I order, how much I actually eat, and if I exercise.

With three restaurant meals a day, no opportunity to work out, and the extra consumption of my Boosts and granola bars, I will certainly gain weight. However, I am not particularly excited about this kind of unhealthy weight gain, since it will be miles outside of my comfort zone.

> *Do you know how much butter*
> *and salt they add to restaurant meals?*
> *Why do you think North Americans have become so FAT?*

I pray that Mother will allow me to use the gym in our hotel. I believe that compromising is key: if I eat big meals

– maybe even dessert – then she will have no choice but
to lighten up. There are several mandatory core exercises
and yoga stretches that I *must* complete daily – they are
not an option – but what if I am refused access? Will I
be forced to secretly work out in our hotel bathroom?
Anxiety overwhelms me again, only this time it is much
worse than when I went to Quebec all those months ago.
I know damn well that I will not be granted the luxury of
skipping meals this time.

August 2, 2012

Oh, my God.
I really do need help.
There is someone else inside of me typing these words.

"Do not let it consume you."
           It consumes me.
                  "Do not let it frighten you."
                        It frightens me.

"Do not let it control you."
           It controls me.
                  "Do not let it suffocate you."
                        It suffocates me.

"Do not let it harm you."
           It harms me.
                  "Do not let it influence you."
                        It influences me.

"Do not let it confuse you."

It confuses me.

"Do not let it weaken you."

It weakens me.

"Do not let it define you."

It defines me.

"Do not let it become you."

It *is* me.

"Do not let it win."

I.

Already.

Have.

August 11, 2012

Arriving home from a family vacation always puts me in the same state: teary-eyed, sleep-deprived, and hungry.

First off, I simply cannot stand New York City. It really is full of overweight people selling fatty, greasy food on dark, smelly streets piled high with garbage. How one can genuinely enjoy a vacation in such a place escapes me completely.

And just as anticipated, my family and I fought daily, and I was constantly being pressured to eat like everybody else…. I was not allowed to exercise at the gym – despite my constant pleas – meaning that I confined myself in our small hotel bathroom to perform my daily core exercises and yoga routine. I think that my family suspected what was happening behind the bathroom door, and this frightens me deeply.

As if things weren't already terrible enough, I was forced to drink two Boosts and eat three granola bars *plus* the three restaurant meals daily. I have never had so many panic attacks before in such short order. One night at a restaurant, my mother's classic disappointed glance made me feel so guilty that I had no choice but to order and completely devour a milkshake – a fucking milkshake!

I will never forgive you for that.

It tasted heavenly, but the demon goaded me into a ten-minute crying session in the ladies' room shortly afterwards. Luckily, I gathered enough strength not to purge, even though Ed repeatedly tempted me to.

All you had to do was stick one little finger down your throat and problem solved.

Oh, and I took twenty fucking minutes to eat a damn granola bar in the hotel room; picking apart every little oat, chocolate chip, and nut cluster in my hand, and savoring the taste slowly, because that is what crazy fucking people do, and clearly I am fucking crazy.

August 13, 2012

You are the fattest little bitch I have ever seen in my life.
I do not think I have ever met anyone who eats so much.
You must be absolutely delusional
to think that THAT *was perfectly normal.*
You are a fucking freak; a fucking fat,
lazy, hideous freak with zero self-control.

I am so so sorry I did not mean to binge I swear but
you see my game tonight was rained out and all I did
earlier today was go on a bike ride so I didn't know what
to do I came home and instead of going to the movies
with the soccer girls I went home and worked out more
than I should have I do not know why I did it I suppose
it is because Ed told me to but then I felt guilty so I
went downstairs and opened the fridge door and saw
leftover cake and for some reason I took out a piece and
very slowly at first put it in my mouth then I realized
how delicious and foreign it tasted so I ate it yes I ate
the whole piece but it did not stop there because I then
turned to the cupboard and ate a handful of nuts and
then a granola bar because you know I do not want to
lose weight I cannot lose weight so I ate I ate I ate too
much now I feel full and scared I am really really scared
someone please help me never to repeat this because now
I have to go work out again even though it is late at night
and everyone is asleep I wonder if I will ever sleep tonight
or if I will spend it worrying and scolding and worrying
and scolding.

August 15, 2012

Since I am "young and athletic" with a typically high metabolism, my therapist reassured me that it is likely that my body will burn off the extra calories, as if it is now restricting weight gain similar to the way my mind does. Not that I discovered that I have lost weight at today's assessment or anything. But I have only gained about three pounds, bringing my current weight to 110. Despite the limited progress, I still feel pride and relief flush over me when I see the little numbers on the scale increase weekly.

I have just fifteen more pounds to go until I reach my starting weight – before I encountered Ed. Of course, I still feel remarkably hesitant about returning to 125 – and immensely hesitant about gaining *even more* weight after I get there – but I am faced with no other choice. I'm at a crossroad: gain weight or be hospitalized.

Mental improvements this week have been noted as well. I have finally put an end to planning my meals and snacks beforehand. This accomplishment may seem rather insignificant, but the fact that I am beating Ed little by little, day by day, is quite uplifting. Ed may still be in the lead by an impressive amount, but now I am on the scoreboard. I may not be ready to throw a punch just yet; I am still the opponent who has been knocked out effortlessly and fallen to the ground. But at least I have regained the wherewithal to get up.

August 21, 2012

Total weight gain: 15 pounds.
Current weight: 112 pounds.

After speaking with my therapist about long-term options, I am reassured. Because of my quick progress, which has been better than that of most eating disorder patients, my appointments can move to every two weeks once school begins. She also suggested starting light workouts at home or joining my friends for fun physical activities *if* I eat more to compensate and continue to gain weight. Little does she know that I have never stopped my workouts at home. Either I am impressively good at being secretive, or everyone around me is completely unobservant.

I worry about missing school every two weeks for these appointments. After all, how many dentist excuses can one offer in a single year? Surely others will construct their own theories about my regular disappearances and weight fluctuations, as though they are all competing to see who can come closest to the truth.

All I would like for my graduating year is to be able to join sports teams and to have a positive experience without all eyes on me for once. Is that too much to ask? I suppose I can't blame my peers if they stare; I am a wreck. I am like the walking dead.

August 24, 2012

"You see, Danah? Do you see how skinny you are
compared to all of your friends?" Mother asked as I
showed her the pictures from the beach last weekend. We
were looking at a photo of all of us girls in our bikinis.
While I can admit that – despite my weight gain – my
shoulders are bonier than those of the others, that is only
one petty detail. Take a look at my unreal six-pack abs or
my long, lean legs.

"God, Mom, I am not *that* much thinner," I replied.
"I mean, look at what happens when I cover our top
halves with my hand. See? All of our legs are practically
the same size!"

Mother shook her head slowly and stared at me for what
felt like hours, her eyes betraying disappointment, fear,
and anxiety. "No, Danah. No, they are not."

> *Oh, please.*
> *The bitch is just being delusional.*
> *If anything, the only difference*
> *is that your legs are a little chubbier.*

Ah! Now that Ed has pointed that out, I kind of see it….
And my leg muscles don't show as much as those of some
of my athletic friends. Fuck. That's probably because of
those fifteen fucking pounds of fat that I had to gain.

Angry and upset, I storm out without uttering another
word to Mother. I hide in my room to cry and to work out.

August 28, 2012

I am always so fucking embarrassed during soccer games.
Why? Well, first off, I never get played. It's evident I am
no longer strong, fast, or even sane enough to be trusted
on the field. To make matters worse, I embarrass myself
further by compulsively stretching behind the team bench
during the entire fucking game. Why do I do this? I don't
have a choice; Ed forces me to.

> *Yeah, no shit.*
> *Since you are not on the field,*
> *you are going to have to move that lazy ass somehow.*

I dread going to my games because of the shame, the
embarrassment, the anxiety, and the tears. Just last week, I
was the final player to get put on with only a few minutes
left. Since I really don't give a fucking shit anymore, I got
pissed at my coach and showed him attitude, forcing a
fight with him on the bench. I cried my fucking eyes out.
Even when I – miraculously – played for five minutes, I
was crying my eyes out like a big, embarrassed baby. The
second the referee blew his whistle to signal the end of
the match, I grabbed my bag and darted out of there with
such speed that I managed to surprise myself.

I didn't think I could stand to look at either of my asshole
coaches ever again, but my selfish, fucking mother forced

me to attend all of this week's practices and a game, even though all I wanted to do was hide in my little stretching cave and bawl.

I remember a time when I used to be so very talented and passionate about soccer; I really did have potential to shine.

> *But then I came along.*
> *I showed you what is important in life.*
> *Fuck soccer; it is all about the extensive workouts.*

I remember voluntarily playing in the backyard every summer day with my dad and sister. I remember smiling and laughing and having confidence in my skills. I remember being invited to train with the regional team. And now? I don't even look at a damn soccer ball unless absolutely forced to.

August 30, 2012

Continuing the trend of gaining approximately two pounds a week, I have now reached 114 pounds. As a reward, next week – the first week of school – I don't have an appointment. From now on, *if* I maintain steady progress, the appointments will spread out from every two weeks, to monthly, to every six months, and so on.

Although that seems to be such a long way off, I have faith. Even the doctors and the therapists believe in me; they say that my motivation to recover thus far has been quite outstanding. Clearly, I *really* despise Ed and long for him to be ripped off of my back.

But now with school starting, anxiety has started to surge within me again. I have begun to worry, feeling increasingly nervous about school messing up the timing of my meals and snacks and workout schedule. This year will certainly be a tough challenge for Ed and me. I'm apprehensive that he will see this as a golden opportunity – presented on a silver platter – to beat me.

September 3, 2012

"Is that all you are having on your sub?" my friend asked me. I looked down at my six-inch whole-wheat sub with cheese and veggies, and for a moment I actually felt a pang of regret. My growling stomach indicated that I really should have at least ordered a foot-long if I wasn't going to have any major source of protein for the remainder of the day.

But that flash of regret vanished almost immediately because I looked over at the heavy subs of my friends – one of them had Meatball Marinara, for crying out loud – and knew I had made the right decision.

"Yeah, well, you know, I don't really like cold cuts anymore," I mumbled. "And I didn't want to risk feeling sick on the rides if I got a foot-long, you know?"

There was a brief silence before my Meatball Marinara friend spoke dryly.

"Yeah, no. I need food."

Everyone laughed hysterically, as if it were the funniest goddamn thing anyone has ever heard. I smiled weakly and then proceeded to eat my sandwich in silence.

September 7, 2012

Great. Perfect. Just my fucking luck. This year's gym class involves a great deal of fitness. Next week, for example, we are already faced with a beep test, a twelve-minute run, and strength assessments.

Yes, baby!
Imagine how fit you will be!

Although this news may excite Ed, it actually worries me, as I believe it will meddle with my weight gain. To some, this may seem like an easy fix: Why not simply cut back on the home workouts?

The solution is far from that simple, as my home workouts are designed each day for specific muscle groups and the different aspects of fitness. If I were to eliminate one at random, then clearly, that aspect would greatly suffer.

I am terrified that health class will rekindle familiar feelings and thoughts from last year, since healthy eating habits and daily exercise were the constant topics of discussion. Why must health classes *always* revolve around this material? Why don't teachers feel the need to cover the issues that all of this "healthy eating" gibberish causes for teenagers? Can't they see that the more the facts are impressed upon our vulnerable minds, the more likely we are to obsess over the details? Yet I wonder if this is true for everyone, or am I am the rare exception; a lost cause.... Did I take all of the numbers too seriously, causing myself to venture too far on my own?

> *Baby, you are not on your own.*
> *You will always have me by your side.*

Thankfully, I won't have to juggle both rep soccer and club volleyball this year, since I plan to choose volleyball – assuming that I make the team next week. Once again, concern edges in as I worry that even the slightest change in my schedule will cause my weight to shift.

I've promised myself to avoid checking the scale on my own, but with all of these new changes, I'll have no choice but to keep a constant eye on my weight.

September 12, 2012

I need someone in my life to tell me that I am beautiful
and strong and sexy, and someone to scare the demon
away when I no longer have the courage to.

September 15, 2012

As predicted, the arrival of the new school year did,
in fact, hinder my progress over these past two weeks.
Luckily, I didn't regress completely and lose weight. I just
managed to maintain my previous gain. Apparently, my
body requires a bigger change than the addition of one
extra granola bar.... But what else on my diet can I shift
around? This is where everything becomes trickier, since
it is becoming increasingly difficult to distinguish my
own voice from Ed's when I reach for another yogurt or
a larger plate of pasta. And unfortunately, it has become
much easier to surrender to Ed's orders and spare myself
the post-meal drama.

"No, that is too much food, you will gain unhealthy weight!"

One habit that my mother would really like me to change
is my consumption of the *exact* same thing daily, but she
cannot fathom how difficult this would be. I will begin to
panic and stress about whether some meals or snacks from
previous days were considerably heavier or lighter.

"How will this affect my weight?" is my perpetual

question. And frankly, this process has become both physically and mentally exhausting. My portions are already too big for a person of my small size; I feel full so easily and quickly now, but I need to keep eating. Then the more I eat, the more I panic, and the more I will exercise afterwards to burn off the excess food.

I
am
trapped
in

a
vicious,
ceaseless
cycle.

September 24, 2012

I really wish I could take a blissful break from it all – some form of recess from all the food, bickering, and confusion. I try *so* hard at times to block out the sounds and commotion in an attempt to have some reprieve from my conflicting thoughts, but it is impossible to do so. My mind will not keep still and the pressures that I face daily refuse me any peace and serenity.

The recovery process was so much less painful and confusing at the start – nearly effortless! All I needed in order to gain weight was one Boost a day. Now, due to the adjustments that my body has made to my new diet, it is much more complicated. I am desperately struggling; I am drowning, failing to break the water's surface. I feel myself beginning to lose hope and slip down into the hole once again.

> *So why not just put yourself out of your misery?*
> *Surrender to me, and you will never fall again.*
> *It is only up from here, baby.*

What is the point of trying anymore?

When is it time to give up?

> *The time is now.*

September 27, 2012

I take back what I said many months ago about dying.

I do not wish to die;
I wish to
F
A
L
L
into
a
deep
slumber
and
to

not
wake
for
a
very
long
time.

September 28, 2012

Haiku to Ed

You dragged me away
Where no one can hear me scream
And you locked the door.

October I, 2012

My weight took a *giant* leap today.

Back to where it all began…

125 pounds.

But it is not over yet,
so I am told….
Will it ever be?

October 5, 2012

Fairytale

You stumble across a hole, inviting you under.
You inch toward a demon, booming as thunder.

Slowly, it consumes your body and your soul.
Slowly, it controls your thoughts and your goals.

Dragging you from your feet, it sweeps
you from the floor.
Dragging you from yourself, it shuts and
locks the door.

Scramble to your feet; chase the demon away.
Scramble to your freedom; make the monster pay.

Your efforts are useless; it stays with you forever....
Your battles are hopeless; it leaves your side never.

To blame oneself...that is honest, no?
To fight oneself...that is madness, so?

Perhaps it is too late to take another swing.
Perhaps it is too late to crown another king.

October 6, 2012

MUM AND DAD KEEP FUCKING WATCHING
ME SCRIBBLE AWAY IN MY NOTEBOOK AND
I CANNOT EVEN FUCKING DEAL LIKE WHEN
WILL THEY LEAVE ME ALONE DO I HAVE ANY
SEMBLANCE OF PRIVACY IN THIS HOUSE I
BET THEY COME INTO MY ROOM WHEN I AM
OUT TO READ EVERY DIRTY WORD WHAT THE
FUCK IS WRONG WITH THEM!!!???

October 7, 2012

Despite being back to what I weighed a year ago, my
mental state couldn't be more different from what it used
to be. Just twelve months ago, I could eat three times
more than a normal person my age without having one
silly little doubt, fear, or threat cross my mind. Now? I
go into panic mode the second I swallow one damn bite
more than I should have.

The same goes for my exercise routine. Just last year I
could sit on my ass practically all week – apart from
playing soccer every now and then – without feeling
a hint of guilt, regret, or unease. Now? I find myself
plunging into panic mode the instant my routine faces a
change.

Last night, for example, a massive power outage hit before
I could exercise because I had procrastinated and been

lazy during the day. Not only was I scolded severely by Ed for hours and hours, but I also had a severe anxiety attack as I paced in my bedroom figuring out how to burn off my food intake for the day.

You see, the weather was far too shitty for an outdoor bike ride or jog, and since the damn power was out, the treadmill was not an option either. To make matters worse, I had already done *all* of my home workouts for the week, so I really was fucked either way. My mind raced wickedly, until finally, I decided to create a workout on the spot. Sounds like a good plan, no?

NO.

Since the workout had not been preconceived or written out, I didn't know when to stop – or rather, I was not *allowed* to stop. I was upstairs in my room shredding it out on the floor for over two hours.

My parents knew.

My sister knew.

Everyone knew.

They tried to call me down to join them for a movie – their foolish attempt to reel me in – but I ignored every shout and knock at the door, just as I consistently ignore everyone's efforts to send me down the road to recovery.

Fuck recovery.
Fuck everyone.

Fuck the damn demon for causing me
to feel this goddamn crazy.

OctobeR 10, 2012

Chasing Recovery

I see it through the changes in the mirror.
I taste it through the bitterness of the grub.
I feel it through the pinch of extra skin.

But am I close enough to
reach out and grasp it?
Or will it fall through my
skinny fingers as I miss it?

Climbing the hole – up or down?
Jabbing the demon – right or left?
Fighting the disorder – conquer or defeat?

OctobeR 14, 2012

About a week ago, a tiny splash of red appeared in
my panties. I actually thought it might have been my
imagination, or maybe just my tired, hopeful brain
imagining the near impossible. But the next day, the tiny
splash of red returned! It disappeared a few days later, as
though it had never been there at all. But it was – and its
significance is

H   U   G   E.

My nurses have now scheduled my appointments monthly! Although I am, of course, relieved and ecstatic, I feel as though everything has been moving so quickly since I reached the magic number – 125. First, my mother stops purchasing Boost, then this spotting appears, and now I don't have to visit the 8th floor until November? Don't they see that I am easily as capable of crashing as I am of rising? Why am I being so rushed?

But wait…. This is what my heart has been hankering for all along: independence and recovery. Clearly this whole problem is more complicated than I thought. Although my body may show signs of recovery, my mind still pleads desperately for Ed to set me free and for someone to throw me a lifeline and pull me out of the pit. The recovery process is long and exhausting. I fall back down into the hole time and time again. I do not believe I will ever truly escape.

> *What are you* really *trying to escape from?*
> *I reassure you, I comfort you,*
> *and I provide you with love and care.*
> *Your parents, on the other hand,*
> *tear you down, belittle you,*
> *and impede your happiness.*

October 20, 2012

Why?

      Why did you choose to torture me instead of
somebody more beautiful?

You were screaming signs of imperfection and vulnerability.

Why?

      Why do you continue to haunt me instead of
somebody with more virtue?

You will remain my prisoner;
my hostage under my sole command.

October 23, 2012

The Boost in the fridge has completely disappeared and
the supply will not be replenished. Today is the day to end
that consumption as well as my daily abdominal and yoga
exercises. Although it took a very long time to reach this
point, I give credit to my mother for *finally* talking some
actual sense into me the other day. Hammering away at
the nearly indestructible shield Ed has constructed around
me, my mother was eventually able to crack it slightly.
Some traces of positivity and light were allowed to enter.
Mother had the determination and strength to probe my
mind even before I did.

She reassured me that eating more on days that involve

intense or frequent exercise is normal and necessary. Although these words may sound familiar, Mother used to approach me often to discuss the issue while I was in the midst of eating or exercising, which was a rookie mistake. Tensions, emotions, and hormones run insanely high for me at those two times; if anyone is to interrupt or distract me, I break down and cry.

Mother says she doesn't want me to obsess about either gaining or losing weight; she would simply like me to *maintain* my new weight and to start eating "normally" again. How could I refuse this request? My body and mind have both been in such distress recently due to my constant overeating, that actually eating less sounds extraordinary!

I agree.

Now that I am open to the idea of consuming in attempt to achieve maintenance, I must not only eat less, but exercise less too. That's why my daily workout had to be put to a stop…. Well, sort of put to a stop. You see, I still perform a couple of exercises nightly for my volleyball fitness program, along with a bit of stretching. However, this routine is just ten minutes, so I view it as acceptable. And after all, I will not be in this stage forever; I will eventually cut it out once the volleyball season ends….

Believe what you want, honey; exercise is still exercise.
I told you that you could never get rid of me.

I feel the demon's fingers fumbling to grasp my ear, as he places his lips close to speak into it. But for once, Ed has become too weak to take control. I am doing the right thing this time. I know it.

November 1, 2012

Although I am absolutely baffled as to how it happened, I stepped onto the scale on the 8th floor today to discover a brand-new number starring back at me: 127.2. This weight gain means that I have now passed my starting weight from before I encountered Ed.

> *It also means that you are FAT.*

For once, *I* am in the position of authority. Even at roughly 127 pounds, I can truthfully say that as I look into a mirror, I admire the strong, athletic figure looking back at me.

The doctors have promised to keep our appointments to a monthly schedule now, and that I will be free soon enough if I gain just a few more pounds.

> *Wait, what happened to maintenance?*
> *You are already so heavy!*
> *Just imagine what you will look like at 130.*

Will I really be free after "just a few more pounds?" All the whispering in my ears increases my doubt…. Just last week they said I was allowed to *maintain*, and the story has already changed. Will the doctors *or* the disorder ever release me?

November 8, 2012

Lately, it seems as though my mind has been playing dirty tricks on me again. It's as if Ed's method of rebelling against my body's recovery is to fuck greatly with my emotions. I have never had such anger or stress issues before. Since the beginning of grade 9, I have had temper tantrums and anxiety attacks almost daily. Thankfully, these explosions occur in the privacy of my home. I'm afraid that one day, I will lose all control in public when something doesn't go my way.

I just crack.

I scream. I cry. I whine. I groan. I throw. As though the whole world has shut down beneath my feet and the *only* way back in is to have an extreme outburst. It would be easy to blame it on the substantial leap from grade 8 to grade 9, but realistically my temper tantrums are only school related about a third of the time, give or take. The other incidences, well…

I blame the disorder.

If I don't have enough time to eat my morning snack, I freak out. If my family insists on joining me at the gym, I howl and sob uncontrollably. The ridiculous list goes on and on. Admittedly, these mental breakdowns started to occur during the first stages of the demon's attack last year, but the fact that they are returning more often now convinces me that Ed has returned with a vengeance and is warming up in the corner, ready to fight. The demon is back to haunt me and drag me down into the hole again....

And all I can do is cry.

NovembeR 24, 2012

Heavenly Father,

I apologize for distancing myself from you lately, even though I suppose that in these tough times, I really should be reaching out for your wisdom, forgiveness, and courage. I pray that you forgive me for all the sins I have committed in the past few months, but really, my back is against the wall. I honestly can't help screaming, crying, being angry, and causing stress in my family. Please understand that this horrible person is not who I am. I am being controlled by a relentless, dark disorder and suffocated by the demon in this collapsing pit.

Please, Protector, save me from this end; don't allow me to fall and to meet this tragic fate. I miss your sunlight, your warmth, and your shelter. I beg you to instill in me the ability to rip the sorrow away.

Christ, my Lord, what do you seek in return? All that I have to offer is a kind sincere soul that will spread only positivity from here on…. At least, I will try to with every ounce of strength that remains within me.

December 4, 2012

Current Weight: 129 pounds.

"Relax – maintain this new weight."

"Keep gaining until your period returns."

Listen to me; the other voices don't know shit.

"Stop being so obsessive about your eating choices."

"Just a few more pounds; you are almost there."

You have gained more than enough already – lose five pounds.

Then lose another five.

Then lose another ten.

Then lose it all.

December 10, 2012

Big news today! My period has returned. Clearly, these weight-maintenance adjustments have been working well for me. I am so glad to be back on track and to being much closer to finding myself again.

On a more unfortunate note, I have been wondering lately if my sickness is spreading through the family like some infectious, poisonous virus. My older sister has always been slightly curvier than I. In fact, her body initially contributed to the development of my disorder because she was a perfect example of how poor eating habits catch up with one's body. Even so, the insensitive twit now has the nerve to constantly ask for my health advice. In her ridiculous quest to slim down, she wants to know how I lost all of the weight that I did! She wants to know how? Get a fucking eating disorder – that's how.

I will attack her with pleasure.

I see my early habits beginning in her: skimping on carbs, hitting the gym every day, planning her meals, counting calories, measuring portions, doing research, and finding inspiration. It is as though she is literally *trying* to acquire an eating disorder. How has she not seen the traumatic impact it had on me? She must be blind, or even worse, she's already been invaded by a demon. If so, it is a long road to recovery, rest assured. And no one deserves to battle similar struggles as I had.

I think I am taking this all so seriously because seeing my (old?) self within her awakens memories of my previous habits: all her talk about weight loss, all the time she spends at the gym, and all of her measuring.... Why am I not doing those things anymore? Shouldn't I be exercising vigorously and being picky about my food choices too?

Yes, follow your sister.
She knows what is right.
She has me by her side.

I feel as though I should blame myself. After all, it was *my* vulnerability that allowed Ed to attack. *I* allowed the disorder to spread.

December 22, 2012

Today, I officially said good-bye to my food blog as I signed off of my Tumblr once and for all. I was absolutely astonished – and elated – at the comments of a handful of my followers when I announced that my exit was due to Ed slowly finding his way back into my mind through all of the pictures of health foods.

"I wish you the best in your recovery. Stay strong."
"I had no idea that you, too, were struggling
with an eating disorder!"
"I hope to see you return some day soon,
but for now, take all the time you need."

Upon creating this blog, I really didn't imagine making the number of friends that I was lucky to meet. You see, the "recovering" community on Tumblr really is something special; people from all over the world come together to show support, seek advice, and to praise one another. Free of harsh judgments or criticism, the account really was my method of escape.

Then why did you quit it, and blame ME?

I didn't have a choice! Recently, I came to the realization that I should try to eliminate all potential triggers in my life, and seeing as the blog was one of the first signs of my disorder, it had to go – unfortunately along with my thousands of followers and friends.

Maybe I will return to the Tumblr community one day. And hopefully, I will return *alone,* without Ed pulling me by my leash and whipping me until I bleed.

January 4, 2013

I am feeling amazing so far this New Year.
Like I am revived.
Like I have risen from the dead.
I am muscular and toned and slim and sexy.
The mirror is finally showing me what I want to see.

Wait.
Suddenly, the mirror is laughing.
Suddenly, I have drawings all over my body,
Circles surrounding fat and stretch marks and acne.
Where did that beautiful, confident person go?

She
Fell
Into
The
Hole.

January 19, 2013

Last night I dreamed that I had forgotten to work out all
day and that I had these intense midnight cravings so I
strolled on down to the kitchen and ate an entire apple
pie yes an entire fucking apple pie probably because my
damn stomach really was growling when I finally went to
bed but I really just woke up terrified and sweaty and with
tears in my eyes I literally almost screamed thankfully I
didn't because that would have woken up my parents but

I was just so afraid that the dream was actually real but luckily it wasn't I mean I would never forget to work out and then eat an entire apple pie right like someone please tell me I would never commit such a disturbing crime as that.

January 27, 2013

With the arrival of the New Year, I can confidently check off one item on my resolution list: to perfect my weight maintenance at 129 pounds! I am so, undeniably *proud* of myself for beating the disorder and reaching my weight goal.

> *You think you have beaten me*
> *just because you have gained a bit of weight?*
> *I AM STILL IN CONTROL OF YOUR MIND.*

Are you, really, Ed? Just last week I ate a slice of cake and a cake-pop! I don't feel extreme guilt or anxiety anymore when I indulge in a restaurant or take-out meal because I truly believe I have finally grasped the meaning of "everything in moderation."

> *But does that make you a winner or a fat-ass?*

Okay, so clearly disordered thoughts still creep into my head – quite often, actually. And sure, I still measure certain things – many things, actually. And yes, I continue to time myself while eating at home – outside of home, actually. But having gained the strength to (occasionally) beat the disorder, I can now hear my own, genuine, healthy thoughts far more distinctly.

I am not required to return to the hospital for another six months, and at this point, all I can hope is that my regular periods will continue until then.

January 30, 2013

Either I was invested in fitness and food from a young age, or I really was born all fucked up inside the pit with the demon by my side. As I was flipping channels on the television earlier today, I came across a show that caused me to think about my childhood. The extreme weight loss show, *The Biggest Loser,* really was one of my favorites at a surprisingly young age. I vividly remember binge watching multiple episodes on cable TV during the summer. Clearly, I must have had nothing else to do, but the fact that I kept returning to shows like that and *The Last 10 Pounds Bootcamp* must mean that it is simply in my nature to care this strongly about living a healthy lifestyle, no?

Yes, that makes perfect sense to me.

Me too, Ed. I'm glad we can agree for once.

February 15, 2013

Lately, I have been quite agitated about the whole "healthy" trend that everyone seems to be pursuing: eating right, working out, *talking* about eating right and working out…. It makes me feel like the disorder is returning to taunt me; that even when I think I have pushed it out of my head, it lingers.

I scream at the top of my lungs when people around me discuss weight and fitness. I want to yell at them all to WAKE UP and STOP CARING before they stumble into the dark hole and are attacked by the demon. I want to save them before it's too late. Is Ed searching for new victims and workers, or have I become completely paranoid?

February 19, 2013

Haiku to Ed

I squeal and seek help,
Failing to escape your grasp.
I give up once more.

February 26, 2013

After tumbling down the stairs and injuring my lower back quite badly, I have been dumped miles away from my comfort zone into a whole new realm. I am in far too much agony to attempt even the smallest amount of exercise.

Ed keeps telling me that my muscles will turn to jelly, and I will gain weight even after just two days of rest. So what will happen in a week if I have still not recovered? How do I go from feeling so strong when beating the disorder to feeling so damn weak when Ed is winning?

The   demon   is   still   yet   to   exit   the   ring.

March 7, 2013

Luckily, my injury didn't last long at all, and I have flown back into the warmth of my safe place.

Yes, and flown right back into the warmth of my arms.

Miraculously, I have managed to maintain my weight of about 130 pounds, too! But there is still a constant reminder that my quest for recovery is not complete just yet, since I have not had that little red spotting in my panties in months. I understand that my period has always been somewhat irregular due to my active lifestyle, but what if this is a sign that there is still more room to gain?

Stop saying that!
You are already so fat!
How can someone like you be proud to call yourself fit?

CAN YOU GET OUT OF MY HEAD FOR A DAMN SECOND WHILE I THINK?

I AM *HELPING YOU THINK!*

NO, YOU ARE CONFUSING THE SHIT OUT OF ME.

YOU ARE ONLY CONFUSING YOURSELF.

Why must the voices in my head continue to soil my clean thoughts? I was doing so well. Just two minutes ago I wrote how about how proud I was for maintaining my new weight! How can my body have come so far in the process of recovery while my mind is still so fucked?

Most of the time, I am able to beat the thoughts – to momentarily flick them out of my head – but their frequency has kicked up a notch lately, or so it seems.

March 10, 2013

Restaurant outings with the family will be the death of me. Even now, I am constantly watched and whispered about. It makes me feel as though they *still* don't trust me, despite the obstacles I have overcome to make it here. They make me think that all my progress is worthless.

"What is she ordering?"
"Is that all she's getting?"
"Why don't you try this?"
"Try this."
"Drink this."
"Eat this."

I want to crawl under the table and cry die,
while my busy mind races through thousands and
thousands of thoughts
as I stare at the menu.

What is more likely to be fattier,
the pasta with pesto and seafood or the pasta Alfredo?
Should I order vegetarian,
or will the others complain about my "lack of protein?"
Will I be judged for requesting
no sauce at all on my food?
Maybe a salad would be the best option…
but I am afraid I will get hungry.
Okay.
I can have this dish if I do an extra workout
and eat a fat-free breakfast tomorrow.
Sound good?
Yes.

No one will ever truly understand the chaos that occurs
in my poor head, often before I have even stepped into
the restaurant. Usually I go online beforehand to search
through the menu and pre-determine my order to ensure
that I eat the cleanest, most harmless meal.

Even so, I always – *always* – come home and feel the same exact thing:

> guilt and guilt and guilt and guilt,
> so I stress and stress and stress and stress
> and I work and work and work it off
> until Ed is satisfied, and my stomach feels empty.

March 14, 2013

Haiku to Ed

> I am always torn
> Between your comfort and threats.
> Why victimize me?

March 22, 2013

If there was some part of my body I would be overjoyed to change, it would surely be my thighs. They are far too large, and not in the intimidating, athletic way. They are simply covered in too much fat and skin.

I feel queasy just looking at them.

(Did I feel this way yesterday?)

Someone get the fat off of me.

(What is wrong with a bit of fat?)

Burn it off.

                    (Burn?)

Snip it off.

                        (Snip?)

Just get it off of me.

                            (With pleasure.)

April 3, 2013

My   mind   is   caught   in   a
perpetual   turmoil   of
   ups   and
        downs,
          ups   and
            downs,
                ups
and
             downs.

      I am stuck on a constant

D
O
W
N
F
A
L
L

with the demon, and there is no escape.

April 8, 2013

I never used to feel so shy, small, and hesitant in front of a large group of people; normally, I am a natural communicator, able to speak to and lead any crowd.... This situation, however, was far different from any other.

"Danah," Ms. said softly to me, before gesturing toward her grade 8 health class, "how about telling them what you went through?"

I gulped as she continued.

"You can really open up – as long as you feel comfortable. I'm sure the girls would greatly appreciate your story and your honesty."

I didn't know where to start. I couldn't concentrate; all I could do was wonder why the fuck I had agreed to speak about my "disturbed" past to a younger class.

All eyes were on me. I had to start somewhere. Luckily, I managed to beat around the bush about what exactly is wrong with me for quite a while; I spoke very broadly about the importance of mental health, surrounding yourself with positivity, and just how crucial self-confidence is.

This is easy, I thought, until my partner – a girl my age – asked to speak about her previous family troubles. Unexpectedly, she got to *my* topic even before I did.

"I have been taking diet pills since grade 6," she said, completely taking me by surprise.

"You have?" I whispered back to her, and she responded with a nod of her head.

All at once, I felt compelled to tell the whole truth, and nothing but the truth, because if she could come out with this frightening truth, the least I could do was utter the words that I had been dreading to say for so long.

"I developed my eating disorder last year, in grade 8, the same age as you guys are now." I held my breath and waited for the roof to collapse over my head, or for the floor to cave in beneath me, but when nothing of that sort happened, I continued.

"It really is crazy to think that one day, you feel perfectly fine and sane and healthy and content with yourself, and the next, it's like…it's like…" I searched for the right words, until I remembered that I had just promised myself to tell the entire truth. "It is like a demon has invaded your mind and has turned your world completely upside down."

I took the silence as my cue to continue. The words poured right out of me. I covered everything from start to finish – the triggers, the hospital, the voices, the fears – until tears welled in my eyes and I couldn't continue. I looked into the crowd of girls and saw tears in the eyes of some, which only made me more emotional.

"Wow, thank you, Danah," Ms. said faintly, clearly stunned by how honest I'd been and, of course, by how fucked up I am.

"Does anyone have any questions for either of the girls?"

Hands shot up, and my partner and I spent the next hour or so providing advice and support to whatever questions the girls had regarding mental or physical health.

I don't think I will ever forget the experience, and frankly, I hope that those girls don't either. I would never want them – anyone, for that matter – to fight a similar battle. If they have to, I pray that they do exactly what I suggested, which was to be honest, get help early before they are out of control, and not to give a fuck about weight or body image or sex appeal.

I only wish I could do the same.
How can I expect to help them,
when I can't even help myself?
How can these girls place even
a sliver of trust in a hypocrite like me?

May 6, 2013

My sister and I got into a fight today and she called me fucking anorexic, even though she knows damn well how much I fucking HATE being called anorexic. What a cheap little shot, Sis. You know, maybe when Ed attacks *you,* you will wake up, grow up, and realize that anorexia is no fucking joke. And maybe then, you will have a little more fucking sympathy, you dumb bitch.

> *Don't be concerned about her.*
> *I will seek revenge on my own.*
> *No one shall ever call you anorexic again.*

May 9, 2013

Am I mentally regressing every time I open up this journal to admit to my deranged thinking and messed-up behavior?

May 20, 2013

Track season has finally begun at school. Normally I wouldn't waste time worrying about the impact of school sports on my weight. But since I am a long-distance runner,

I'm certain that the extra calories I burn will cause a drop in my weight. Should I quit the team or just eat more? I really don't want to do either. I am so sick and tired of the disorder causing me to avoid fun, whether it be going to the movies with friends or playing a game of soccer.
I have become a robot. I go to school. I return home. I eat. I exercise. I sleep. I repeat. There is no room for amusement. Ed has no patience for laughter and diversion.

June 2, 2013

Stepping into the weight room for the first *real* time, feeling small, weak, and foolish, was unquestionably intimidating.

What are all these bars for?
How does this machine work?
Am I doing this exercise right?

I hope to eventually get the hang of it with the help of Google, of course. Suddenly, I find myself wanting to gain a new reputation as a body builder – and as a force to be reckoned with.

June 10, 2013

Fuck.
I don't have time to go to the gym today.
But today is a gym day.
I have already completed all of my home workouts.

There are no other workouts for me to do.

This is so stressful.

Why is this so stressful?

I am pacing nervously in my room and I do not know what to do.

Repeat a home workout?

No.

Then I would have to repeat all three

That would be too much exercise.

Right?

Fuck.

So what do I do?

I cannot do cardio because I already did cardio this week.

Fuck.

Why do I have to go to this stupid family event?

Why didn't I go to the gym this morning when I had a bit of time?

Oh, right. Because my parents were fucking sleeping.

Why are they so selfish?

Please help.

I don't know what to do.

What workout do I do?

Should I take a rest day?

No.

I don't even need Ed to tell me how bad an idea that is.

June 19, 2013 (15th Birthday)

I woke up this morning convinced that I would automatically feel better about myself. After all, I am an entire year older…. Shouldn't I be more developed?

You should be, but you are not.
Tell me why.
I need to see a list.

My tummy is still too flabby.
My thighs are still too chubby.
My shoulders are still too bony.
My breasts are still too flat.
My butt is still too saggy.

My   mind   is   still   too
                    fucked   up.

I couldn't have said it better myself.

June 20, 2013

Shockingly enough, I managed to come out of my grade 9 graduation with a few leadership and academic awards, and even one athletic award that, to be quite honest, is pretty damn *loser-ish,* if you ask me.

Okay, I sound super spoiled and ungrateful right now, but I can assure you that I really am proud of myself for racking up these awards, and thankful for my teachers of three years who were able to recognize the good in me. You see, all I am saying is that when I imagined receiving an athletic award, I didn't think it would be the Mike Meredith Sports Award that basically rewards positivity and leadership. My good friend won a *real* award for her overall contribution to athletics at my school.

Does this make me a loser? To be honest, I sure do feel like one. This award just proves my lack of actual skill in any sport. Oh, but don't worry, that's okay, because apparently I have a great fucking attitude.

Yay.

June 31, 2013

> *JUST BECAUSE IT'S FUCKING FRUIT*
> *DOES NOT MEAN YOU CAN OVEREAT.*
> *WHO THE FUCK EATS TWO ENTIRE*
> *FRUIT TRAYS ALL BY HERSELF?*
> *GOD, HAVEN'T YOU LEARNED*
> *ANYTHING SO FAR?*
> *YOU ARE SUCH A FAT-ASS.*

Well, I…uh…technically did not eat two entirely by myself…. Okay, yes, I ate a lot of fruit throughout the day, but I needed some sort of fuel for the tournament!

> *WHAT THE FUCK DO YOU NEED FUEL FOR?*

YOU ARE BENCHED EVERY GAME.
FUCKING IDIOT.

July 4, 2013

Is the scale joking right now,
or did you really drop 5 pounds?
This is such excellent news!
Let's celebrate.

I am far too dazed and busy to celebrate right now, Ed.
The numbers on the scale are creating all-out panic as I
scramble to come up with *more* menu additions that will
boost my diet and gain back those pounds.

Or you can think of ways to lose another 5 pounds?

Or you can shut the fuck up, Ed?

Feisty.

I AM SO CONFUSED
AND SCARED.
DO I INCREASE FOOD,
OR DO I DECREASE EXERCISE?
I DO NOT WANT TO ADMIT
TO MOTHER THAT I WANT
TO GO BACK TO THE HOSPITAL,
BUT I DO I DO I DO I DO
BECAUSE I NEED HELP AGAIN.

July 5, 2013

I am such a fucking idiot. Why would I allow Mother to check off the "meal plan" option for the next two weeks of camp? Did I do it to prove to her that I am perfectly fine with eating disgusting, greasy, salty cafeteria food?

WELL, I AM NOT.

Hey, no need to stress.
Everything is going to be okay.
How about we increase our exercise, right?
Oh, and no granola bars during the day for you.
Plus, fat-free meals for breakfast, got it?
You see? Problem solved.
You are welcome.

July 7, 2013

Why can't I have the amazingly strong, athletic body of the professional tennis players that I am currently gawking at on my TV screen? Not only do I envy their bodies, but I really do envy their lives too; they train hard, they eat glorious super foods, they rest well, they inspire others, and the majority of them make a ridiculous amount of money.

Fuck. My life is a fucking joke compared to that. I will never be an athlete who impresses or influences others because I am not a good enough athlete to even make the starting lineup of any of my rep teams. Soccer? Ha! Not since Ed attacked and ruined my passion for the game. Volleyball? Yeah. In a million years, maybe.

I am not experienced enough.
I am not talented enough.
I am not strong enough.
I am not fast enough.
I am not fit enough.

And I will never be.

July 22, 2013

"Danah, Dr. Oz is on!" Mother called from the TV room. I sprinted down the stairs and plopped onto the couch beside her, ready to learn. The show today was, as usual, about weight loss for middle-aged women. But today, it was specifically about what to look for when scanning the nutrition labels on food items and how to plan a balanced, fulfilling diet that wouldn't leave a person craving sweets or wanting to binge uncontrollably.

"You see, this is why we don't just diet in the first place," I said to Mom who was interested in hearing about how to control one's sweet tooth. "Because if you eat filling, nutritious food, then you won't even feel a need to snack."

"Yes, but not all of us have the same self-control as you, Danah," Mom replied. "Besides, you have never really been into eating chocolate and candy and junk food as much as most other people. Consider yourself lucky, child."

"I guess," I mumbled under my breath, before Mom could hush me so she could listen. I listened attentively too, and while I certainly didn't agree with everything Dr. Oz and his guests were suggesting, I realized there was no point in sharing my opinions on the issues; just because my crazy, loaded diet worked for *me* – a young person with the energy, drive, and time to work out for an hour to two a day – certainly didn't mean it would work for those grown adults.

And what kind of fifteen-year-old spends her weekend evenings watching Dr. Oz with her mother, anyway?

July 30, 2013

I have a new obsession, and it is the bulge of muscle on people's legs that appears as they strut on by. I can't help but watch the legs of practically all athletic-looking girls in their tight little shorts, whether they are at the gym or on the street.

Similarly, I can't help but walk back and forth, back and forth in front of my full-length mirror, staring at my own leg muscles and comparing them to my previous observations.

Unfortunately, my legs are often the losers, but I hope that I can use this as motivation and inspiration to work harder and eventually have the best leg muscles of all my friends.

Maybe I should be hoping that these new obsessive thoughts are not considered disordered or controlled by the demon.

August 6, 2013

Should I feel proud of myself for asking my mother to book me an appointment on the 8ᵗʰ floor, or should I feel disappointed that I allowed myself to return to this state? Although her response sounded quite casual, her body language screamed of bewilderment and frustration. I can only imagine the thoughts that entered her mind: *Oh no, here we go again. My daughter is falling again.*

I am desperately seeking answers and reassurance from my therapist. Ever since Ed has begun shouting more aggressively, my thoughts have been in constant turmoil. A continuous battle between Ed and me is being waged. Ed doesn't give me many options. It always seems to come down to either, "eat this and you will *gain* weight," or "do not eat this and you will *lose* weight." Am I really so fragile that it can jump from ups and downs to downs and ups in a matter of just a few bites? Is it my mind that over-complicates the simplest of situations and meals?

Despite the entire fluster, I can sincerely say that I did not once enter a gym or hotel bathroom and secretly work out during our family Vegas trip, which we returned from last night. This is a huge step toward recovery for me, especially when I remember how stressed I was during last summer's vacation. But don't get me wrong. I came

extremely close to cracking many times after we hit the
buffets. But I always made sure to do a couple extra laps
at the pool the next morning....

This is acceptable, right?
Maybe I really should have gone to the hotel gym.
What if I gained a lot of unhealthy weight?
What would Ed do to me?

Oh, trust me. You don't even want to know.

It horrifies me how easily doubt can cause my mind to
flick the switch on me.

August 7, 2013

The elevator shoots me up to the 8th floor, where I shuffle
down the hall, staring at my feet, avoiding the dreaded
EATING DISORDERS sign up ahead. Before I enter the
office, I turn my attention to the familiar painting on the
glass wall just to the left of the bathroom. RECOVERY IS
POSSIBLE, it states in big, loopy, cursive writing, and I
can't help but imagine what this painting would look like
as a tattoo on my body.

I enter the office, grab the little brown paper bag and
plastic container with the orange lid, and slide across
the hall to the bathroom. I sit down and pee into the
container.

Not too much!
You must save some of that water weight
for when you step onto the scale.
They cannot know your true weight.

My hand shakes. I stare into the mirror. I see my old self
with razor-sharp cheekbones and the puffy, blue bags of
an insomniac under my eyes. Is it just my imagination?
Or have I really rewound that far?

I exit the bathroom, place the brown bag with my pee-
filled container onto the office desk, and enter my room.
I do not need the receptionist to remind me which one
is mine. The process is all too familiar. I step out of my
own clothes and into the hospital gown. This is when my
breathing always quickens. I clutch the cross around my
neck and gaze up at the picture and frame above the scale.
I recite the poem that is beautifully printed and silently
chant the mantra and prayer. After I finish this ritual, I
open the door slightly to indicate that I am ready.

The nurse walks in and greets me but I am too nervous to
respond. Instead, I step right onto the scale, shutting my
eyes tightly. I hear her pen scribble the numbers that have
appeared on the screen. I open my eyes and face the truth.

As predicted, I lost just over five pounds. My heart rate
has remained normal, but I must complete more tests to
get to the bottom of my disappearing period.

I cry.

A lot.

Well, how could I not? I always cry nowadays; my heart has turned to mush; my mind has turned to chaos. I even cry when my therapist attempts to comfort me, saying that she doesn't think this weight loss is a devastating issue. She blames it on the fact that "everyone is more active during the summer."

> *What a lovely excuse, as long as the heat is off me.*

But was that the truth? Was what she said the same as the notes she typed into my file? Was it the same information that she gave my mother afterwards? Why didn't I deny her silly excuse? Why didn't I throw Ed under the bus and tell her that the dark, aggressive thoughts have been returning? Perhaps it was because she reassured me that it's only natural to have to battle the lingering thoughts every now and then. It is only when I let these thoughts control my actions and prevent me from seeking help that "the problem becomes grave and needs to be revisited."

> I do not
> think I
> can gain
> these five
> pounds back
> this time,
> I really
> don't.
> I do not

want to

put in

the effort.

I do not

even want

to

care.

I am

testy and

I am

tired.

August 16, 2013

I swear to God, Mom takes her sweet-ass time on purpose
when we go on our fucking walk every evening with the
dog, even though she knows I still have to eat my evening
snack by a certain time. She allows the dog to stroll along
and sniff every damn blade of grass and pee on every
damn bush or tree, and I am just standing there shuffling
my feet on the spot – because I not allowed to stop
moving – and *praying* for us to hurry along so I can get
back by the correct time and still have my ten minutes to
eat, but this fucking selfish woman only cares about what
the damn dog wants.

"Danah, slow down!" she barks whenever I think *Fuck
it* and begin my fast pace down the road toward home.
Normally, it is at this point that I begin to cry because for
some damn reason, I have absolutely zero control of my
emotions, and I seem to think that crying is the answer

to everything. So, yes, I cry and cry and cry and cry, and when I look at my watch and see that I really will be late, I run and run and run and run home to fill my face, and then I go up to my room and smile because food makes me happy. ☺

(and stressed.)

August 22, 2013

I would be a complete liar if I said that these past couple of weeks haven't been difficult for me. In fact, they've been pretty similar to the dreaded summer of 2012. I have been cooped up inside all day; no biking, no running, no volleyball in the backyard.

I scold myself for being so foolish and careless. Why did I have to lose those five pounds? Why didn't I think of the consequences?

I want those five pounds back
and I want them NOW.

No, you do not.

I want my period back
and I want it NOW.

No, you do not.

I want to be free from the
disorder and I want freedom
NOW.

No, you do not.

August 29, 2013

I hate it when my fucking schedule is messed up, but I
know that my demon hates it even more. I was supposed
to do my third home workout today, which takes about
an hour and a half, but Mom randomly decides to drag
me around doing errands all day despite my pleas to
go home. Then suddenly, she also decides it would be a
splendid idea for the family to go out to this disgusting
Indian restaurant for dinner – WHICH I DID NOT
PLAN FOR – meaning I didn't get home until 7:30
this evening, but since I made plans to sleep over at my
friend's place in thirty minutes, there is no fucking time
to do my full workout. I do not know what to fucking
do…. Sure, I could skip the sleepover, but Mom would be
beyond pissed at me if she found out that I skipped it to
secretly work out in my bedroom.

You should have known.
Blame yourself, not your mother.
It is your fault you failed to plan in advance.
You have to anticipate that these kinds of things will occur.
Rain? Snow? Unexpected plans? Sudden change of events?

Fuck, I really wanted to go to that sleepover. But Ed is right. It *is* my fault; I had some fucking nerve to sit there and blame my mother. Okay, it is only 8:00, so maybe if I work out now, Mom will still be willing to drive me at 10:00. Fingers crossed.

September 2, 2013

September is what I have been craving for months now; the autumn weather, the start of volleyball season, the excitement of Halloween, the cozy atmosphere, and most importantly, the start of another school year! Although tomorrow is only a half-day, I feel the angst and unease of the butterflies fluttering in the pit of my stomach. I am so eager for tomorrow's arrival, as I will walk into my new high school with high expectations regarding classes, clubs, teams, parties, and, of course, boys.

I don't want a repeat of my junior high years – constantly falling for the same stupid guy and having my heart broken repeatedly. But I do want to experiment and have fun this year. Above all, I am definitely searching for my first real hookup, and perhaps even my first boyfriend.

But what right-minded guy
would love a fat girl like you?

SeptembeR II, 2013

Why must my weight affect everything I do? I went from
feeling so undeniably carefree and thrilled about the new
school year to feeling exceptionally nervous at my most
recent *voluntary* hospital appointment. I stepped onto
the scale to find my weight at 125 pounds – not too far
off my highest peak. Of course, I am yet to see the return
of my period. The last time it came back was when I was
130, so it's no great mystery what I have to do if I ever
want to achieve this crucial step in my recovery.

Damn! How I despise the process of gaining weight. It
brings back such uncomfortable memories of stuffing and
then hiding myself. I suppose that losing weight would
bring back even worse memories now, wouldn't it?

SeptembeR 19, 2013

Ed has somehow managed to turn even the most
mundane task into an exercise routine. Take the shower,
for instance—

Scrub harder.
Wash the fat away.
Dry your hair vigorously.
Yes, work those weak arms.

Or walking to and from school—

Don't you dare cut a single corner.
You cannot walk even one step less than yesterday.
Pump those arms and speed up those feet.
Who cares who is watching?

And yes, even going to the bathroom, where I must perform a squat, instead of simply sitting. I am not allowed to sit down right away, especially after I eat. I must walk, or stand for at least ten minutes, or until Ed is satisfied…. Sometimes, he is not satisfied for hours. The bottoms of my feet ache, but I am forbidden to stop. When will this endless exercise come to an end? Will I spend my entire life constantly preoccupied with working out? Will I ever be allowed a moment to simply stay in bed?

September 20, 2013

All of my friends are devouring the bags of chips and popcorn that I brought over as we watch this terrible movie, but all I can think of is what meals and workouts I will do tomorrow. I see them eyeing me suspiciously as my pile of junk food remains untouched.

September 28, 2013

Walking off of the field for the very last time with the group of girls that I have grown up with for practically ten years was far easier than I expected. I really just wanted to get the fuck out of there; I was tired of being surrounded by all of this negativity and competition. Truthfully, it was a breath of fresh air to realize that I was finally free of this poisonous team the second that final whistle was blown.

I wonder what the last two seasons would have been like without Ed at my side. After all, being miserable and benched for the past two summers was due to Ed sucking the passion right out of me. The disorder made me weaker and slower on the field. How could I blame my coaches for not putting me on? Sure, they definitely could have handled certain situations a whole lot better, but realistically, no one is to blame here but Ed.

Ed is always the one to blame.

> *Yes, go ahead and blame me for everything.*
> *Blame me for the beautifully toned body you now have.*
> *Blame me for the new healthy lifestyle*
> *you will forever call your own.*

Okay, okay, okay. Maybe Ed did help me to achieve some positive things in life, but they were no compensation for all of the tears shed, all the relationships lost, and all of the optimism blown away.

October 1, 2013

I have just spent the past four hours browsing through the hundreds of eating disorder websites to see just how accurate this bullshit information could be. Shockingly – and terrifyingly – it was far more accurate than anticipated.

And

                That

                              Scares

                                  Me

              Beyond

Belief.

Main Types:

1. Anorexia Nervosa→ low body weight; intense fear of weight gain; distorted perception of shape; limited calories; excessive exercise, severe health problems

2. Bulimia Nervosa→ bingeing and purging; lack of control; food restriction

3. Orthorexia→ obsession with foods one considers healthy; avoiding foods in the belief that they cause disastrous, harmful effects on one's body and overall health

Common Symptoms:

1. Skipping meals and rarely eating; constantly making excuses

2. Overly restrictive diet of health food

3. Only eats and prepares own meals

4. Withdrawal from social encounters – especially those involving the consumption of food

5. Perpetual talk and complaints about weight, diet, exercise, and goals

6. Preoccupied by thoughts surrounding food and exercise

7. Checking the mirror throughout the day; distorted body image

8. Tooth enamel loss, thin hair, weak nails, chest pain, swollen stomach

9. Eating extremely slowly

10. Eating in secret; fear of eating in public, or being rushed and stared at

11. Feeling ashamed, guilty, or disgusting after eating

12. Calorie counting and obsessive thoughts

13. Adversely affected by the media, super models, diet blogs, and advertisements

14. Listing good and bad foods; excessive meal planning

15. Rigid linking of meals to specific times; other rituals such as only using a certain cup or plate

16. Behaviors focused around food preparation and planning; shopping, cooking, reading recipes and nutritional guides

17. Repetitive body-monitoring behaviors; pinching oneself, weighing oneself

18. Body concealment; wearing baggy clothes, changing style dramatically

19. Lying about amounts of food and exercise

20. Rearranging food on plate and cutting food into small pieces

21. Denying hunger; focusing on self-control

22. Prepares elaborate meals for others, but rarely consumes them

23. Extreme sensitivity to the cold

24. Loss of menstrual period in females

25. Fainting, dizziness, fatigue

26. Depression, anxiety, moodiness, irritability, low self-esteem

Do I tell the doctors
at my next hospital
appointment that I still
possess many of these
symptoms...?

I
Never
Know
What
Is
The
Right
Thing
To
Do.

October 5, 2013

I just had the biggest fucking brain fart I spaced so badly
I don't even know why I started eating my evening snack
at 6:45 instead of 6:50 so I did not even get a full hour
to digest my big stupid fucking dinner I am such an idiot
why did I not wait those five stupid minutes oh my God
it is times like these that I really fucking hate my life and
realize just how stupid I really am.

OctobeR II, 2013

Today was...

> The last time I hope to step into the
> Eating Disorders hallway on the 8th floor.

> The last time I hope to acknowledge
> the *Recovery is Possible* painting.

The last time I hope to take a pee test
and place it in a brown bag.

> The last time I hope to meet with
> the nurses, doctors, and therapists.

> The last time I hope to recite the poem
> above the scale before weighing in.

> The last time I hope to feel
> my heart drop at the numbers
> that appear before me.

> But it will not be the last time I encounter Ed.

Although I am elated today that my counselor declared I'm officially on the right track, that I don't have to attend hospital sessions any longer, and that they plan to take me off of their books for good, I am still reunited with my good old friend Uncertainty. I have gone from feeling confident and appointment-free to practically begging to return to the hospital in a matter of days; I am certain it will happen again. Hopefully, it will not be anytime soon, but realistically, I know that won't be the case. The hole will never become easier to clamber out of. The demon will never quit. The disorder will never wholly disappear.

Will I be able to fight it all?

I am capable of shrugging the voices off most of the time, but will I ever enjoy complete recovery? When will I be strong enough not to hear the voices at all? My muscles are beginning to ache. I have grown too tired of chasing recovery in this never-ending race.

> *Maybe if your legs were not weak as*
> *fucking jelly, you could keep up!*

October 12, 2013

Haiku to Ed

I bid thee farewell;
A good-bye to the *8th* floor,
And hello to Ed.

October 15, 2013

Why do I care so damn much about what everyone else is eating, how everyone else is exercising, and if everyone else is mentally healthy? I am by far the worst in my friend group when it comes to being judgmental; I love to find faults in others, and oddly enough, I think that I subconsciously believe I am doing it for a better cause.

For instance, I may take a look at some random girl – or even a celebrity – that my friends all rave about for having the perfect body, and I will automatically shut them down by saying "She is far too skinny." Or my friends will tell me what they had for breakfast, and I won't hesitate to tell them "That is not nearly substantial enough in quantity *or* quality." Honestly, I feel for my friends sometimes; certainly, my behavior must be irritating, but I can't stop, no matter how hard I try. I guess I'm trying to prove to my friends that I no longer have an issue with food, exercise, and body image….

But does all this constant criticism and talk only fuel their suspicions?

October 31, 2013

Haiku to Ed

We spook the children
But the demon wants to play.
Happy Halloween.

November 6, 2013

I walked into the shawarma shop with Daddy – actually
with the intention of ordering a sandwich for once – and
immediately, my eyes lit upon the bloody raw meat in the
back of the shop being sliced and diced and placed onto
the large rotisserie spit.

My eyes darted away and I even had to take a seat, face
the window, and tell myself to breathe.

"Danah," Dad called, snapping me out of my fog. "Come
tell the man what toppings you'd like on your shawarma."

"Daddy, I don't want one anymore," I mumbled, not even
bothering to turn around. I didn't want to see his peeved
expression.

"What?" he asked. "I can't hear you. Come here."

I turned around in my seat, careful not look at the
meat being prepared in the kitchen. "I don't want one
anymore," I said, much louder this time.

"Why?" Daddy snapped. "You wanted one before we got here."

"Uh, yeah, I guess, but I am not very hungry anymore."

"No. You know what? Come here and order. I didn't drive here for nothing. You asked for it, and you're having it. Come *here*."

The man behind the counter stared rudely. When I didn't budge from my seat, Dad rolled his eyes and waved his hand in my direction, shooing me away.

"Fine, whatever. Just get her chicken on a whole wheat pita with cucumbers, lettuce, peppers, and spicy mayonnaise."

"Ew! Dad, what the *fuck?*" I shrieked, not caring about my bad language in a public place (or the fact that he would probably punish me when I got home). Dad whipped around. His eyes were threatening and his hands shook with anger, but I continued anyway.

"If you are going to order for me, at least get it *right!*" I didn't give a shit if my attitude was lousy. I was pissed. "You know I can't stand sauces!"

Fuck. Tears welled up in my eyes. What is *wrong* with me?

You?

What is wrong with HIM?
Do NOT let him walk all over you like that!

"But I…I…already put the mayonnaise on," the man stammered. "Would you like me to start over?"

"Yes, please," I breathed, suddenly remembering a little thing called manners. I sat back down, ashamed of myself, and avoided Daddy's angry glare.

I ate the shawarma when I got home to please Dad, who is still not talking to me, and felt sick to my fucking stomach afterwards. I am disgusted with myself.

And so am I.
You little bitch!
How could you devour that
when you saw the bloody meat?
I hope you enjoyed it while it lasted,
because that is the last shawarma you will ever eat.

November 16, 2013

I don't understand why my family is so fucking stupid. Let me explain. You see, on Wednesday we always have hamburgers for dinner, but I hate hamburgers because they don't fill me up enough and I dislike big hunks of meat. I saved the damn seafood and veggie pasta for a reason. I labeled the Tupperware for a goddamn reason. My name was on it. I took a sticky note and wrote my damn name on it. But my fucking mother took it to work anyway. Selfish bitch. And just last week, the exact same thing happened with the leftover stir-fry I had set aside. But for some damn reason, my idiot sister took this as an invitation to stuff her fat-ass face with it, leaving me only a couple of spoonfuls.

"That is more than enough for you, Danah. Just chill."

I gawked, horrified. "More than enough!? That's barely enough for a damn squirrel, let alone *me*. And no, I will not 'chill' because I am perfectly in line. YOU are the one who fucked up."

"Why are we even fighting over this right now? It's just food. You're *psycho!*"

"I AM NOT PSYCHO. YOU ARE JUST A SELFISH BITCH!" I screamed at the top of my lungs, wishing the entire world could hear me. My sister began to laugh. I began to cry. I stormed up to my room and cried and cried and cried.

November 18, 2013

My friends are more athletic than I am.
My friends are more cheerful than I am.
My friends are more loveable than I am.
My friends are more beautiful than I am.
My friends are more intelligent than I am.

My friends are
better than I am
in every way possible.

I disagree, darling.
You work out far more than they do.
You eat far cleaner than they do.
And that is all that matters.
Never forget that.
Never.

November 24, 2013

I am still so uncertain when it comes to food vs. exercise.
Am I still eating to gain weight? Or is the part of my life
that always had me fighting off the demon behind me
now?

Oh, so naïve...
You can never surpass me.

I am continuing to eat a substantial amount—

Yes, too much.

I am also maintaining my extensive workout regime—

Not nearly extensive enough.

So essentially, this is balance, no?

No, this is all a big, treacherous

G
A
M
B
L
E.

The only thing that would make everything crystal clear is the return of my period…. But what if I am permanently fucked, and it never comes back? What if Ed has scared it off forever? Even my period has taken its turn at running away to hide!

> *Do not even think about chasing it.*
> *Tracking it down will do no good.*
> *It is long, long gone.*

Despite all of my current confusion and anxiety, I believe the mental side of things is improving. Ed is still here – right beside me, watching over exactly what goes onto my plate and how much is sweated off – but *I'm* the one who most often gets the last word.

December 3, 2013

I pranced down the stairs, fully intending to whip up my usual healthy breakfast, when an amazing aroma met me.

Eggs.
And spinach.
Sizzling in the pan.
Wrapped up in a lovely omelet.

Dad gestured me toward the dish without a word.

Wait.
Why was I considering this?
Oh, yes. Because it is perfectly *normal* to eat an egg omelet.
I kept reassuring myself, as the warmth soothed my throat.
I devoured it in minutes.
And went back for seconds.
But who cares?
This is healthy too.
Right?

December 3, 2013

Never again will I eat an egg omelet for breakfast; I felt terribly sick afterwards, both in my stomach *and* my head.

(Ed was not pleased to say the least.)

> *And clearly neither were you.*
> *You see, your body does not*
> *even want that crap.*
> *All of that grease and oil....*
> *Yuck.*
> *Just imagine it*
> *sitting in your stomach.*
> *You should feel ashamed.*

December 9, 2013

"All right, Danah, I am heading out to the grocery store now. Are you coming?" Father calls from downstairs. A smile appears on my lips, and my step is lively as I sprint down the staircase, excited for another weekend trip to the store. Honestly, I *adore* shopping for food; it really is one of my favorite pastimes. There are so many delicious and nutritious options to choose from, so many beautiful colors to take in, and so many new health foods to try.

I also love this Saturday morning routine because I genuinely enjoy spending time with my dad. I'm fairly certain that he would prefer me *not* to tag along with him because I always cause him to spend far more money than anticipated. Hey, it's not my fault that health foods are so ridiculously priced. We spend far more time than he anticipates as well. For example, I spend at least fifteen minutes in the granola and cereal aisle alone, comparing the nutrition facts of my favorites to some new ones I have in mind. And once I finally make my decision and place the item or two – or three, or five – in the cart, I automatically start thinking how I will enjoy it for breakfast tomorrow. I might use a quarter cup of it as one of many toppings on my smoothie bowl. The possibilities are endless!

Today, I am wildly grateful to shop for practically anything my heart—

and your demon—

desire.

December 19, 2013

Daily Workout:
* In Addition to Home/Cardio Workouts or Practice

Volleyball
10 single leg bench squats
10 single leg bench lunges
1-minute bear crawl
1-minute spider crawl
10 neck raises

100 Abs
10 push-ups
10 raises
10 scissors
10 flutters
10 V crunches
10 rolling sit-ups
10 Russian twists
10 toe taps
10 elbow to knee crunches
10 twist crunches

Yoga
10 sun salutations
10-minute stretch

December 25, 2013

Ed scolds me sternly for indulging in a slice of cake this holiday evening at my cousins' usual get-together.

"But it's *Christmas!*" I protest, not even bothering to hide my fear. He whispers ugly threats in my ears and growls through his teeth; he plots the punishments that he will inflict upon me once I return home.

Planks?

Push-ups?

Squats?

All of the above.

The list is infinite.

*Oh, and let's not forget about
the calf raises and crunches, shall we?*

His creativity knows no bounds.

*You are in trouble, my dear friend;
prepare yourself.*

The worst is yet to come.

I wish the voice in my head would subside for one merciful evening. Is it wrong to have made an exception for the special holiday that is Christmas? After all, it only comes once a year....

That is once too often.

Now I begin to scold myself too. Just imagine. All of this unnecessary turmoil and fury could have been avoided if my mouth hadn't fucking salivated at the smell of the rich chocolate-banana combination. If my greedy hands hadn't reached out for that slice. If I hadn't laid eyes on my mother's disheartened expression when I initially replied "No, thank you" to my aunt.

But I did all of that.
And now,
I must live
with the
consequences.
Ed, give me
your best shot.

Ha! Don't tempt me, little girl.
I will do so with pleasure.

January 3, 2014

New Year's Resolutions 2014:

1. Obsess less about diet!

2. Get period back for good!

3. Achieve proper balance between food and exercise!

4. Love yourself, have a positive body image, and be more confident!

5. Avoid weighing yourself!

6. Care less about what others may think!

7. Eat fewer animal products, but still eat in bulk!

8. Continue to improve in volleyball!

9. Read and write every day!

10. Project a better attitude!

11. Be grateful for everything you have!

12. BELIEVE YOU CAN BEAT THE DEMON AND YOU WILL DO IT!!!

January 12, 2014

I do not want to be hasty or melodramatic, but perhaps Ed has snuck back into my life, only in a different form. Yes, Ed has taken on the form of social media again – Tumblr, to be exact. Lately, I have been spending an absurd amount of time scrolling through the glorious yoga and health food blogs. Tumblr was a mutual friend of ours before, for it is what initially introduced me to Ed, only *that* encounter was extremely negative. I am using Tumblr in a positive manner this time around, I swear! My excitement is growing daily as I brainstorm new recipes and attempt new and challenging asanas, but I fear that perhaps my excitement is becoming obsessive....

> *Oh yeah, like how?*
> *Stop exaggerating.*

Well, for one thing, I have started to plan out my meals again – usually at breakfast, as that is where I have most of my new and exciting ideas.

> *So?*
> *Who cares?*
> *Plan all you want.*
> *Planning is organization.*
> *Organization is good.*

For another, these "ideas" are preoccupying my daily thoughts....

In class.

At home.

E v e r y w h e r e.

I don't want to head back down into the hole; I want to steer clear of the downward spiral that is the disorder. I want Ed to let me enjoy these beautiful blogs and bloggers, whom I idolize *without* any risk of losing myself again.

January 20, 2014

Haiku to Ed

I plan to attack.
I must take the demon down;
Kill you in your sleep.

January 28, 2014

My body flowed with ease, lightly and beautifully. From one delicate lift and fold to the next, I was creating a story with each asana. I had never felt more confident about my yoga practice until today, when I nailed the basic – monumental for me – crow pose. I felt lovely and strong. I now have a new reputation to create for myself this New Year: the yogi.

February 1, 2014

I was feeling amazingly strong and sexy at gym today, squatting and bench pressing, until suddenly, a blonde bombshell walked in and drew the complete attention of all the males in the room. The few pairs of eyes that had actually been on me immediately turned to stare at this glorious new figure. And while she was a new face at *this* gym, she was clearly experienced in the weight room, with her sculpted back muscles, toned arms, and firm butt. She was beautiful, to say the least, in that deep-cut tank top and patterned workout leggings.

My
Heart
Sank.

I looked in the mirror in front of me, and analyzed myself with my ratchety top bun, baggy Nike shorts, and volleyball T-shirt. How embarrassing. I left without even finishing my workout, too ashamed to be seen in the same room with someone like her.

That's okay.
You know I will make you finish up at home.
Don't even think about complaining or procrastinating.
You want to be as fit and striking as she is, right?
Well, let's get to work!

February 6, 2014

A doctor's appointment is approaching, and what do I do best in these situations? Stress, of course. I launch directly into complete panic mode; I ponder the thousands and thousands of questions related to my weight, period, and mental well-being.

Have I lost weight?
  Can the doctor see right through me?
      Will there be consequences for not having my period back?
          Would I ever be considered for readmission into the hospital?
              DO I NEED HELP AGAIN?

While I have increased the quantity of my three already extremely loaded meals, I have decided to practically eliminate snacks from my diet again.

Why have I done this?
  Was this my choice, or Ed's?
      How has this affected my weight?
          IS IT THE RIGHT THING TO DO?

If I were to say that I never get hungry between meals, and *that* is the reason I am skimping on the snacks, I would be lying. I really would be. I don't enjoy having to wait for the next meal, even as I hear my stomach growl, but a little patience never hurt anyone…right?

Right.
The growl of your stomach is music to my ears.

But   what   does   it   sound   like   to   *me?*

As much as it kills me to admit it,
I feel like I need help again.

Do I take the chance of asking for
it, and risk pissing off the demon?

February 10, 2014

I was frantically rifling through old photos in my albums
in a last-minute attempt to string together a friend's
birthday gift when suddenly, I stumbled across a photo
from about two years ago that I had tucked into a small
pocket at the back of the album.

I don't think I'll ever be able to forget the appalling sight.

I can remember the moment I discovered it as though it
were yesterday. My mother had forced my sister and me
to pose for a photo before we all left for a sushi restaurant
with some family friends. I was wearing a fitted floral
dress, while my sister was wearing a simple striped T-shirt
dress that hugged her curves in all of the right places. The
differences between the two of us were outstanding. My
sister appeared to be genuinely happy; her cheeks were
flushed and full of color and life, her smile shone brightly,

and her outfit had the perfect amount of sex appeal. The second I looked at myself, however, a shriek escaped my lips. I was utterly terrifying to look at; pale as a ghost, sickly thin as a skeleton, and lifeless as a vampire. I shoved the image back into the pocket and vowed never, *ever* to allow myself to look like that again.

I really had no clue that my appearance had been that alarming. All this time I thought that my case really wasn't that serious. But the picture literally made me look as if I might drop to the floor and fucking *die* at any moment.

And judging from the expression on my face, it seems that I wouldn't have minded if that had happened.

February 19, 2014

126.   126.   126.   126.   126.
  126.   126.   126.   126.   126.
    126.   126.   126.   126.   126.

What does this mean?

> *Well, to me, it means you are*
> *at least 36 pounds too FAT.*
> *But on the bright side, it also means*
> *you have lost two whole pounds!*

Okay, okay, okay, but only dropping two pounds is not totally devastating and life altering, right?

Wrong.

I sank lower and lower into the chair in the doctor's office as she threatened to strip me of my home workouts, *yet again.*

"I would like to see you reach that 130 mark, Danah."
>"I don't want to see you slip back into your old habits, Danah."
>>"I would like to hear that your period has finally returned, Danah."

Since when do we care what that bitch thinks, anyway?

MAYBE I SHOULD START
CARING WHAT SHE THINKS.
I AM SCARED AND LEFT
WITH NO OTHER OPTIONS.
I CANNOT GO BACK TO THE HOSPITAL.

I CANNOT.

I CANNOT.

I CANNOT.

I CANNOT.

*Jesus, who knew two measly pounds
would put you into this much of a pickle.*

I should have known.
I should have known not to trust Ed
with disguising himself as the "harmless" food blogs.

I should have known.
I should have known not to trust Ed
with creating longer, more intense workouts for me.

I should have known.
I should have known not to trust Ed
with convincing me to eliminate snacks completely.

I should have known.
I should have known not to trust Ed
with loading my plate with only fruits and veggies.

Fuck you, you little bitch.
You take that all back RIGHT NOW.
I AM trustworthy and I AM your friend.
Please understand, I only want what is best.

That is pure bullshit, and you and I both know it.

Anyhow, I reluctantly told my doctor I would try my
hardest to gain four pounds and reach that goal weight.
She nodded her head in support, but I could see the
disapproval and doubt in her eyes. I could hear the doubt
in her voice as she replied, "You have six weeks to do it."

At this point, I was practically in tears, fighting the urge
not to run from the room and cry in fear, anger, and
confusion. I couldn't even find the strength to ask her
just what exactly I should do to satisfy her in six weeks.
What should I add? What should I eliminate? And most
importantly, when would this battle finally end?

I   thought   I   was   permanently   at   peace.

February 22, 2014

"Danah, come on. Have some of my big cookie from the cafeteria. You used to love these last year!" my friend exclaimed at morning break.

"No, it's all right, I have my three water bottles."

"Are you sure you don't want a snack?"

"Yeah, don't worry. I have to drink my water to feel full, anyway."

I remember that brief, yet significant conversation clearly. It was the conversation that really pushed my friends over the edge because I completely exposed myself as the girl who had an eating disorder. The next day I was called down to the guidance office to address my "issue." The next few months were the toughest of my life.

I still find it difficult and rather awkward to reflect on that bitter time, but it's interesting to see the major differences. It is almost comical how I was so reliant on water back then to satisfy whatever cravings I might have encountered during the day. Now, I find myself consistently dehydrated. The only time I ever drink is after I exercise, or if I bother to fill a small cup to go with my meals at home. This may seem like it *should* be enough, but clearly it isn't. My frequent headaches, fatigue, and dark-colored pee are proof of that. I know that water is vital to one's health. Trust me, the vegan blogs I follow constantly remind me of that, but for some odd reason I cannot just reach for a glass, even when I am thirsty. In the back of my mind, I fear that by drinking too much water, two things may occur:

1. The obvious; I will have to go to the bathroom far too often.

2. I will use it as a way to fill myself up once again.

March 8, 2014

"But Madame, don't you ever just *crave* meat? Like, don't you just want to sink your teeth into a nice, juicy cheeseburger?"

I glared at my idiotic classmate.

He looked back at me, amused. "What?" he mouthed, as I rolled my eyes at how truly ignorant some people could be. Didn't he know better than to tempt a vegetarian or a vegan like that? People make their life choices for a reason. Who was he to challenge her?

Madame chuckled awkwardly, clearly feeling uncomfortable.

"*Non, non*.... Really, I just do not like eating or cooking with animal products. It is as simple as that," she replied before trying to change the subject. "And now, class, let us correct last night's homework, yes? *Page huit dans le cahier, s'il vous plaît.*"

But the stupid boy was not willing to move on.

"No, but like, seriously, Madame. Why would you *not* want to eat meat and cheese and fish? Like, your life must be so *boring!*" When the class burst out laughing at this, I had had enough.

"What the hell does it matter to you? Honestly, I just don't understand what business it is of yours. Yes, Madame is vegan. Get over it!"

All eyes were on me, but I didn't care; my embarrassment dissolved the moment I saw Madame mouth "Thank you" at me, before continuing with the class.

March 20, 2014

Tears are welling up in my eyes, waiting to be released, but I am trying hard not to cause a flood. But one by one, they begin trickling out of my eyes, and then a sudden downpour strikes, and I am sobbing uncontrollably while staring at my computer screen.

Why can't I stop crying?

Perhaps it's because I have never felt so understood or represented before, and I never would have guessed that this connection could come from the damn television show, *Skins*. I am Cassie. Cassie is me. The similarities are outstanding and frightening and alarming. Are all individuals with eating disorders this way? Are we all the same, from our screwed-up heads to our skinny toes?

Cassie, like me, thoroughly enjoys touching, smelling, and arranging any food in sight, but rarely does she eat it.

> Cassie, like me, is an expert strategist who fools her rather oblivious and insensitive friends and family; she changes any subject related to food or her disorder, mixes and cuts the food on her plate, and suppresses her true emotions.

Cassie, like me, works hard not only to fool those around her, but to fool herself. Through her constant smiles, she desperately tries to believe that everything is all right.

> Cassie, like me, spends a good chunk of her time walking around observing others and thinking deeply.

Cassie, like me, has a brief moment of consideration that is evident in her eyes when offered food. But she knows better and never gives in to temptation.

> Cassie, like me, secretly hides food in her bedroom closet, to have quick access for binging, or to trick people into thinking she has eaten it.

Cassie, like me, searches for comfort and reassurance from childhood memories and objects, by remembering a time when it was far easier to accept herself.

> Cassie, like me, is paranoid. She repeatedly imagines receiving texts and notes instructing her to EAT, when in reality, this is all about telling herself to do what is right.

Cassie, like me, feels hopeless and alone, for she genuinely would like to think that people want to help and like her, but she is always disappointed by the truth.

> Cassie, like me, is faced with a goal at the clinic of gaining X number of pounds in order to be released for good.

Cassie, like me, is so desperate to change the number on the scale while at the clinic, that she attempts to cheat the system by drinking a huge amount of water beforehand, and placing weights in her panties.

> Cassie, like me, simply wants someone to truthfully give a damn. At her friend's urging, she bravely raises a burger to her lips, and although she hesitates for a few moments, she finally does it; she finally eats again.

And now I am here, sobbing from happiness for her, and sobbing from fear as I realize how identical we are.

Except, for the fact, of course,
that she is a television character.

And I am not.
This is real for me.
There is no director to shout "Cut!"

March 28, 2014

Not many people can say they genuinely enjoy the pain as much as I do:

The heart pumping.
　　The muscles aching.
　　　　The chest burning.
　　The sweat pouring.
The heavy breathing.
　　The music blaring.
　　　　The hearty grunting.
The fabric sticking.

　　　　I love all of it, every sweet bit of the pain.

I crave every juicy chunk of the workout. I used to crave it so much that it caused me to starve myself – to lose myself, to surrender to the demon's commands.

But I think I have begun to understand how to control my thirst for it. Sometimes, I push myself further than I have ever gone before – just for the hell of it, just for the thrill. But now I know when to stop…for the most part, that is.

Sometimes, I lose control if the voices get too loud and powerful, and if I know I cannot win. That's when I push the boundaries and break the limits.

"One more," I tell myself. "Just one more push."

Okay, so this may not be ideal for a recovering eating-disorder patient, but when I think about the reward… damn! There is nothing more satisfying than the reward.

Your six-pack and slender legs thank me, darling.
You are welcome.

April 7, 2014

I used to have so much variety in what I would watch on TV.

Reality shows.
Dance shows.
Game shows.
Comedies.
Sports.
News.
Cartoons.
Fashion shows.
House renovation shows.
The discovery channel shows.

And now?
All I watch is the Food Network.

Top Chef.
Cutthroat Kitchen.
You Gotta Eat Here!
Guy's Grocery Games.
Diners, Drive-Ins, and Dives.
The Next Food Network Star.
Bake with Anna Olson.
Celebrity Cook-Off.
Sweet Genius.
Chopped.

Of course, people who do *not* come from a disordered background probably have no issues with watching a ton of food-related television, but perhaps this is a sign that I am developing obsessive patterns again. *Is* this a sign that I am making my way back down into the hole and into the arms of my demon? I pray that it isn't, and that I simply *prefer* all of these food education and competition programs to the garbage I watched before.

Will I be able to stop myself and turn off the TV when I decide that I have gone too far?

I   doubt   it.

Holy shit, child. You really are paranoid.
You are even blaming me now for your television choices!
When will you learn to take some responsibility,
and realize that I am not the bad guy?

I am not blaming you, Ed.

I am just growing nervous about these shows, is all. Please don't be angry or upset; no one is to blame here but me.

April 10, 2014

A little red spotting miraculously appeared in my undies the other day. I was surprised, but more than that, I was relieved.

"Finally," I whispered to myself, "a sign of proper health."

While this is certainly an indicator of good *physical* health, I find myself questioning my mental state. Even though it has been two years since I first wrote about and admitted my illness, the battle feels eternal; constantly starting and stopping. I am not *nearly* as bad as I was, but occasionally I make decisions and then think, *This is what Ed wants; this is what he needs.*

I cannot allow myself even
one rest day from exercise.
I cannot erase all of the food fears
I have bottled up inside of me.
I cannot give in to hunger or temptation
and indulge in a snack or dessert.

And because of this, I can never expect to attain complete recovery, separation from Ed, and escape from the pit.

Beware, for you have barely changed since we first met.

I am back with a vengeance.
And I am here to stay.

April 22, 2014

I feel as though I can always open up to my mother and tell her anything and *everything* that is happening in my life. Whether I need advice, or whether I just need someone to talk to, I know that she is always there. I am so grateful to have the sort of relationship with my mother that allows for this openness and honesty about boys, parties, friends, you name it.

But there is one topic that I don't think I will *ever* be able to speak truthfully about with her ever again.... Any guesses?

Oh, oh!
I know, I know!
It's me, isn't it?
Trust me, I am not complaining.
I never liked your mother's company much, anyway.

Sometimes, I feel that I really do need someone to talk with about my food and exercise fears and insecurities. Someone who won't judge or threaten me with going back to the dreaded 8th floor. I'm tired of concealing all my secrets in the pages of this journal. I am tired of suppressing my insane emotions and frightening thoughts.

Hey, I am all ears, baby.
Whenever you need me, I will be here.

April 27, 2014

"Let's come up with a definition of a mental illness as a class," my social science teacher said, as he gestured toward the bored kids in front of him. There wasn't the slightest indication of a response from anyone, but my mind buzzed with curiosity as I lifted my head from the surface of the cold, uncomfortable desk.

The teacher was clearly unimpressed. "Well, how about we approach the question this way…. What are some examples of a mental illness?"

Apparently this was easy for the class, as hands shot in the air.

"Depression!"
"Bipolar disorder!"
"Schizophrenia!"
"Addiction!"
"OCD!"

"Post-traumatic stress!"
"Substance abuse!"
"Dementia!"
"Alzheimer's disease!"

The list went on and on, but one crucial mental illness was being left out. I tentatively raised my hand, and with a shaky voice suggested,

"EATING DISORDER."

Everyone carried on as if I had not said anything at all, which was fine by me. I wasn't prepared to face the stares that would come from the classmates who were aware of my dark past.

But as we analyzed the difference between *psychosis* – a mental illness – versus *neurosis* – a mental health issue – I began to question my diagnosis. I have always assumed that the crusade against my demon has occurred due to some sort of chemical breakdown in my brain, but perhaps it is all just a phase…. Maybe I don't have a mental illness after all!

Is this all temporary – and thus a neurosis – or are the chemicals in my brain permanently damaged and unbalanced?

Why do you even care?
Why must you put a label on our love?

May 1, 2014

"Wow, that's new!" my Wednesday night yoga teacher exclaimed, as I lifted my top leg in Vasisthasana and reached for my big toe. A smile immediately appeared on my face. Oh, how delighted I was to get some recognition and praise from the woman I admired so much.

It's because of her that I have developed a passion for the exquisite art of yoga. From the way I move my body to the way I surprise myself every week with small – yet meaningful – accomplishments, these Wednesday nights have become my favorite time of the week.

Yoga is something I will continue to practice for the rest of my life, and something I want to improve at each and every day. I must begin a daily home practice, but research will be necessary. I am still ignorant when it comes to the Sanskrit names, technique, and flow of each asana, but with my determination—

And my persistence—

I believe that I can do it.

May 17, 2014

"But the problem with buying shorts now is that I am going to lose weight over the summer," my sister stated proudly. "So how should I know what size to get?" Immediately, I bit my tongue and resisted the strong urge to slug her in the face. Fuck! What do people not understand?

I DO NOT WANT TO HEAR ANYTHING ABOUT YOU AND YOUR DAMN DIET.

And from my own sister, of all people, who I thought would have grasped this concept by now! She continues to be the culprit; her and her never-ending attempt to lose weight. Why? Why must she strive to have the body of a pathetic Victoria's Secret model, let alone mention it to me? Can't she see how irritated I become?

I let it go this time, but Lord help her if she continues ranting about weight loss, dieting, workouts, gluten-free recipes, veganism, and plans to join me on my monthly food haul to The Healthy Planet.

God, she is such an idiot….

Why do I allow her to annoy me so much?

Truthfully, it's because deep down, I feel as though she is stepping on *my* turf; *I* am the health-conscious sister. *I* am the fit sister. *I* am the one who is knowledgeable about veganism and superfoods.

Why doesn't she just go back to her junk-food-eating, meat-loving ways and stop stealing my vibes!?

Sounds to me like you are the one being selfish.
You can't have me all to yourself, you know.

May 18, 2014

Just last week, I hit the tennis courts and played absolutely amazingly, especially for someone who rarely gets the opportunity to play throughout the year. I was consistent, my shots were crisp, I was moving my feet well, and I was actually having a good time.

But today was the complete opposite; all of my shots either sailed out or drove into the net. I couldn't get to the ball fast enough, and I missed practically every first serve.

WHY CAN'T I BE GOOD
AT JUST ONE FUCKING SPORT?
THAT'S REALLY ALL I ASK.
I WANT TO LOVE TENNIS.
I WANT TO BE GOOD AT TENNIS.
I WANT TO ACTUALLY PLAY TENNIS.
BUT I CAN BARELY FUCKING HIT A SINGLE
BALL ON SOME DAYS, SO WHAT'S THE
FUCKING POINT OF TRYING?

May 28, 2014

Although I have some major doubts, I am seriously considering starting a healthy lifestyle Tumblr or Instagram blog, where I would share recipes and pictures of my beautiful, nutritious breakfasts and videos of me performing yoga, or working out at the gym.

I know, I know. Red flags are springing up *everywhere*. But honestly, I have made such stellar improvements that I really do deserve this as a reward for my strength in the battle against my demon so far. After all, I am mentally far stronger than I was in grade 8 when I first joined the Tumblr community. I should be able to handle creating a blog again without being sucked down into the hole, right?

I guess I will never know until I try…. Truthfully, I am afraid; I'm afraid of what my peers at school may think if they were to find me online, and I am afraid of not gaining enough followers. That last one sounds pretentious, I know, but without a decent fan base to provide you with confidence in your ability to influence them, it's really difficult to continue wholeheartedly.

I'm already getting a head start, snapping pictures of my smoothie bowls on my phone, jotting down my favorite flavor combinations and recipes, and creating my own yoga flows. All I want is to be like those famous, recovered vegans and yogis that people – including me – look up to and trust with their important life questions.

June 2, 2014

I have this nagging fear of death and injury practically every time I leave the house. It started out as a thought that would flit past now and then. I never paid any attention, until I realized that they were preventing me from doing things I normally would adore doing. Even when I ignore the thoughts and carry on with the potentially threatening activity, I am overcome with all the "what ifs" as I picture every possible situation.

What exactly are these situations? Well, they can range from tubing in the lake to riding my bike, or crossing the street, or even sitting in the car.

And every time I imagine being shredded to bits by the motorboat, or breaking my legs and never walking again, or having a truck ram into the side of me, the next thought is always the same: if any of these were to happen, would I ever be able to work out again?

Then I begin to overreact and panic. I become frantic as I look for wood to knock on. I shut my eyes tightly and beg for happy thoughts to erase the vision of disaster.

Sometimes this works. Most times, it doesn't.

Does Ed trigger these terrifying scenarios, or am I just looking for someone to blame for my madness?

June 5, 2014

Surprisingly, I am really quite bitter about this year's school soccer season coming to an end. As it turns out, I really did miss playing. I was surprised at my spirit and skill on the field. Okay, I realize that the level of play is far lower than what I was used to when I played rep, but even against some of the top teams in Toronto, I was a strong force to be reckoned with in defense.

Does this mean I will ever return to my old team? Hell no. But it was nice to discover that I've still got it.

June 19, 2014 (16th Birthday)

My heart sank as I searched through the basement cupboards looking for new reads. I had discovered a pile of books that I hadn't seen before:

How My Teenage Daughter Can Beat an Eating Disorder,
Ways to Prevent Eating Disorders Amongst Your Children,
Understanding Eating Disorders,
The Truth About Life with an Eating Disorder.

Book upon book; page upon page – all about me.

When had my mother purchased these? Had she even bothered to read them? Was I really that drastic a case that she had to turn to some shitty self-help authors for advice? I was flooded with questions, while my eyes were flooded with tears.

Hesitantly, I reached for one and dared myself to scan the pages. At first, it felt as though the paper literally burned the tips of my fingers. Then slowly, the pain subsided, and I spent the next hour sifting through the thick, hardcover books and reading about my demon.

The books were filled with information: basic descriptions of the various types of eating disorders, how to recognize symptoms, treatment options.... It was like someone had analyzed my thoughts; taken a trip into my mind; fully exposed my habits and behavior.

This

Terrifies

Me.

And, of course, this all had to happen on my birthday, of all fucking 365 days of the year.

> *Happy sweet 16, baby.*
> *Now, shut the books and go work out.*
> *Who knows what shit they might*
> *make you eat on your "special" day.*

June 20, 2014

I am one of the few people in my friend group to leave my school's annual Athletic Banquet with no awards. Not one.

Despite my involvement in three major sports, I was unable to snag *any* specific team award or even be nominated for Rookie of the Year. Didn't I join enough teams, or do I just fucking suck at every sport I play? I was one of the strongest players on the soccer and volleyball teams – but obviously not even close to being the best. At tennis, I didn't stand a chance.

At times like these, I really wish I had my *own* sport for which everyone would recognize me. Instead, I am fated to be average at everything.

> *Maybe if you were fitter and faster and stronger you could have won.*

That is where I have to disagree; if this were a competition of physical fitness, I would surpass nearly everyone in my grade. Unfortunately, optimal health can only help to enhance one's skill so much, and then it comes down to raw talent.

June 30, 2014

Do I want to go vegan because I genuinely care for
the equality of all animals, because I actually *prefer* the
alternatives to animal products, or because Ed is forcing
this diet on me?

July 1, 2014

My stomach won't stop growling. Perhaps it's because
I haven't eaten since 3:30 this afternoon and it's now
11:00 p.m. I can't sleep because I am unable to snack.
Why would I eat my last meal at 3:30, you ask? Well, this
summer, my beach training starts at 4:30, meaning I must
leave the house at 3:45. Since I cannot play on an empty
stomach, and since I must work off my dinner, I have to
eat from 3:15 to 3:30.

It sounds ridiculous.

I sound ridiculous.

Three o'clock is lunchtime to some, not *dinner,* but what
else can I do?

> *There is nothing else for you to do.*
> *It is nothing that a nice, tall glass of water won't fix.*

Is this hunger really worth something as petty as not
allowing myself to eat snacks? I understand that, in Ed's

eyes, snacking equals a lack of self-control, but what about how I see it? Doesn't that matter at all?

What a stupid, pointless question.

July 3, 2014

I am going to drop.
I am going to give up.
WAIT.
Did that thought really just sneak past Ed's guard?
Oh, my God.
Yes, it did.
WAIT.
Will I actually go through with it?
WHAT?
No, there is no way I can break this asana.
Just imagine how pissed Ed will be.
He will never let me hear the end of this one.
NEVER.
I regret even thinking it.
Is it too late to take the thought back?
FUCK!
Everything is burning.
My core.
My arms.
My legs.
I cannot do it.
I am going to drop.
I am going to give up.

My heart sinks at the disappointing sight of stopwatch in front of me.

No.

No.

No.

NO.

There is no way I can do this for another two minutes.

What is wrong with me today?

FUCK.

Have I really become this weak?

I thought my abs were stronger than this.

Oh, no.

AH.

I am slipping.

I am scared.

I want to drop.

I think I will.

I think I have to.

Do I have a choice?

HELP.

What is the worst that could happen?

> *Don't you fucking dare, Danah.*
> *Don't be a fucking pathetic weakling.*
> *I will make you do it all over if you drop.*

SHIT!

Okay, fine.

FINE.

I will push myself.

I will not give up – for you.

July 15, 2014

"Ew. What *is* that?" I gagged at the greasy mess of deep-fried food on my friend's plate.

"What? It is from *The Colossal Onion!*"

"So, it's literally an entire onion cut open and deep-fried?" God, my cholesterol was skyrocketing just from looking at that thing.

"Jesus, Danah," he said. "We're at the fall fair. It's practically a crime *not* to order the most disgusting, greasy food you can find!"

"Then, I guess I am just a fucking criminal now!" I snapped back.

"Hey, everything in moderation, right?" he said with a smirk. He dunked a piece of battered onion into some sort of mayonnaise sauce. "Come on, try some," he said. I cringed, waving my hand in protest, and actually had to turn away from the sight *and* the smell.

Honestly, I don't understand why people would voluntarily feed their bodies such *CRAP.* After all, we really do only have one body; it is *essential* that we optimize its performance in every way possible by fueling it correctly and exercising it sufficiently…. Is that disordered thinking? Certainly not. There is absolutely nothing wrong with wanting to spread my love for healthy living and my concern for the well-being of others.

Yes! You go, baby.
Spread the word for the world to hear
Let everyone know that I am yours to share.

July 17, 2014

Constant conflict. I am in constant conflict with the demon.

Weight.

Diet.

Exercise.

Will I ever experience peace in my life? Or will I continue to be toyed with by Ed?

He has left a permanent tattoo on my soul; he resides within me. Lately, I hear him scratching at the door, like a dog, begging to be let inside.

Did you really just eat all that?
Since when did you lose so much self-control?
Keep overeating like this and you will gain weight.
I told you, look at how bloated your stomach is.
You disgust me.
I thought you liked your body.
Why are you still eating to add on the pounds?

Just because something is considered
"health food" doesn't mean it won't make you fat!

Even when I confidently admire myself in the gym mirror, or devour a large bowl of rice, Ed always has something to say. And although I am not happy admitting this, perhaps what he is suggesting is actually fair. I *have* been eating a ridiculous amount lately.... No snacks or junk food, of course, but still a ridiculous amount. I'm constantly feeling bloated after each meal, but I can't stop myself. Ed is right; my self-control has diminished greatly over time. I wonder if this is actually positive or negative.

July 18, 2014

I have finally completed my first original yoga home practice to perform daily, and I am beyond excited. With this, I will gain more strength, flexibility, and balance. I will ensure that I sweat every day. I will focus more on my breathing. I will end each routine with beneficial meditation. I will be a genuine yogi exactly like the ones I marvel at on my computer screen.

Yes, you will be beautiful and lovely and fit.
All yogis have amazing bodies, and now, you will too.

July 19, 2014

I am so frustrated right now because the damn recipe did not turn out like the image on Instagram even though I used the exact same ingredients and measurements like fuck I hate my life so much right now what am I supposed to do with this shit it is falling apart I could just dump it all in the blender or bake it instead of eating it raw or maybe tomorrow I will just wing it ha ha yeah right no wait I really don't want to eat this for breakfast tomorrow morning it looks bad I am so disappointed maybe I should just give it to my sister I hope she wants it because I hate to waste food okay so then which recipe should I make now instead?

August 3, 2014

There is no better way to wish my sister a happy birthday than by making her favorite raw, vegan dessert! Sometimes I really don't mind recipe-sharing with her, although I can get terribly annoyed, watching her attempt to whip up superfood delights like I do. But considering it is her birthday, I have decided to give it a go. For once, I placed things in the food processor *without* measuring, and I did not care what – or exactly how much – went in. My goal was to make it as indulgent as possible. After all, my sister is quite picky, and in her eyes, the more chocolate and peanut butter the better.

The final product looked so positively delicious that I couldn't resist snapping a quick picture before she saw it. As for tasting it myself, well, that was a different story.

There is no way I would have ever *let you have a bite of that loaded crap.*

Loaded crap? It is completely healthy and nutritious!

Sure, the ingredients were fine, but you didn't even measure!
It is for your sister and family, and them ONLY.
You have your picture.
Pretend you tasted it.
Go work out.

But I don't want to work out right now. I want to see my family's reaction when they bite into the delicious cake....

No, you want them to turn it
around on you and offer you a piece.
Selfish pig.

I think I am *far* from selfish, considering all the time and effort I put into this dessert.

Oh, please.
This was all for you anyway; any excuse to be in the kitchen.

August 12, 2014

I think I may be afraid of running on my own again. I honestly used to enjoy running. My weekly jogs were time away from all the craziness at home – and in my head – because they were always so refreshing and satisfying.

Ah, yes, the sweat; the calorie burning; the fat shedding.
I can remember it so clearly now.

Then why haven't I run once yet this entire summer? Every time I lace up, I back out and ride my bike instead. *Why?* Has running become too difficult for me all of a sudden? Has my cardio fitness really gone to shit? Is it because my fat stomach always feels too damn bloated to move? Or do I dread it because I want to avoid the constant competition with myself?

Whatever the reason, it bothers me, because the longer I allow myself to avoid running, the harder it will be to start again.

I used to be such a healthy, happy cross-country runner – I really did. Now I'm just a washout who is afraid to even go on a harmless jog.

Okay, that is not entirely true, because practically every day last week when I was on holiday in Barcelona, I went for a run. But there it felt entirely different. It is far, *far* easier to run when you don't have a destination or time frame in mind, or when the gorgeous views and ideal weather are always on your side. I guess I hoped that, upon my return home, I would be inspired to begin running regularly again. Alas, I wasn't.

> *I don't even want to* think *about that trip.*
> *Yes, you ran every day, but you did* NO *strength training.*
> *Nor did you do your daily yoga flow.*
> *Do you realize how loaded all of those dishes of paella were?*
> *I hope you understand the severity of your*
> *actions and the mistakes we must correct.*

Oh, fuck off, Ed. I enjoyed the food in Spain, and all of the runs and the walks were *more* than enough exercise…right?

Fuck.

No.
No.
NO!

Ed is right again.

No wonder stretching was tougher when I returned home. I probably lost *all* of my hard-earned flexibility!

And no wonder my home and gym workouts were more exhausting. All of my strength must have disappeared during that one week away!

Now I am going to have to work extra hard for the remainder of the summer to get it all back.

August 14, 2014

I feel bad for wasting my time taking pictures of my breakfast every day, but honestly, I adore capturing that perfect image of my heavenly food. I probably spend about thirty minutes every morning adjusting the lighting, setting up the décor, creating the ideal backdrop, and finding the best angle for the picture.

But I don't care.

I really don't.

It is just *so* exciting to see the final images, and while some certainly turn out better than others, I am extremely proud of each and every one. I edit my favorites and arrange them into a collage every month. I label them and drag them into the MY FOOD folder on my desktop. Whether or not I will ever use them in an online blog is still a mystery to me, but this is a new hobby I don't think I could ever drop.

August 16, 2014

"What!? You really don't like *any* sauces?"
"You don't put ketchup or mayo on your burger?"
"Wait, you don't even like hamburgers!?"

"And you, like, *never* eat junk food?"
"Not even cookies?"
"No chips?"

"Jesus, what *do* you eat every day?"
"Salad and fruit sound boring to me."
"What the heck is a smoothie bowl??"

"How about french fries?"
"Okay, you must like pizza!"
"What is your favorite food?"

"So you would rather eat
bananas than bacon?"
"Tofu instead of chicken wings?"
"You are so weird."

My eating habits are a source of entertainment for the campers at my volunteer placement. At first, I didn't mind the attention; it was kind of enjoyable sharing what I love to eat with younger kids who are still stuck in their McDonald's phase. But eventually, I began to feel like a social science experiment. They continued to poke and prod, and soon enough, even fellow counselors joined in the "fun."

But I wasn't lying about any of it; I have simply developed a love for health foods over junk food. It's a shame that the campers cannot see how beneficial this lifestyle is. All they see is a weird girl eating pasta without sauce. At least that's better than seeing a girl with an eating disorder.

August 21, 2014

Ed was constantly screaming in my ear tonight in the gym weight room, as I allowed my inexperience and insecurity to dictate the duration of my workout.

"It isn't my fault that people I know from school are here! I don't want to look foolish! Some of the exercises are embarrassing!" I argued, but Ed couldn't have cared less.

> *Get your lazy ass back on the machines.*
> *No one will give a shit about what you look like now.*
> *They will only see how amazing and*
> *beautiful and strong you become.*

August 30, 2014

The smell of the eggs and bacon cooking on the portable grill both disgusted and intrigued me. I couldn't even remember the last time I ate anything *remotely* similar for my favorite meal of the day.

My friends' smiles as they happily ate their cholesterol-filled breakfasts actually caused me to feel envious about how easily they allow themselves to eat such greasy, unhealthy food. I was pretty okay watching them pig out – until someone brought out several different loaves of bread.

My mouth salivated.

My stomach growled.

I tried to convince Ed to let me have a slice or two. After all, it was past 11:00 a.m. Technically it could be considered my lunch. And this way, I wouldn't have to eat the nasty hamburgers and hotdogs that my friends had planned for later on in the afternoon…. This really was the better way to go.

Good point.
You may have two.

I began to reach for the "English-style Raisin" variety when Ed suddenly snapped, causing me to quickly withdraw my hand.

Are you high?
Do you realize how much
sugar and salt is in that type?

But it looks the most delicious…. Come on, Ed, this is
my only intake until dinner!

Why should I care?
Go for the multigrain, idiot.

I did as I was
told.
I ate two
slices in
about two
seconds.

I reached for two more.
Ed was screaming beyond belief.

The sound was ear-splitting.

But I was hungry.
And my friends were waiting
to see how much I would eat.

I didn't have any other option.
I ate two more slices with a smile.

WHO THE FUCK EATS FOUR SLICES OF TOAST!?
WHAT THE FUCK IS WRONG WITH YOU!?

*IF YOU THINK YOU ARE GOING TO SPEND THE
WHOLE WEEKEND HERE,
YOU BETTER THINK AGAIN, DUMB BITCH.
AFTER THIS FUCKING STUNT,
YOU WILL GO HOME EARLY TO WORK OUT.
YOU WILL BARELY TOUCH YOUR DINNER.
YOU FUCKING FAT-ASS.
YOU DISGUST ME.*

Frankly,   I   am   disgusted   with   myself.

September 1, 2014

Weed makes my fingertips and toes
go numb. Weed makes time go by
quickly, while making my feet move
so damn slowly. Weed makes my
head go 'round and 'round in circles.
Weed makes me see flashing lights on
the field. Weed makes my mouth go
dry; dry like the Sahara Desert. Weed
makes everything that much more
hilarious. Weed forces me to laugh
and laugh and laugh forever and ever.

Weed is good. Weed is
calorie-free. Yes, I have been
doing my research since the
moment I giggled my way
home. And get this: in the
long run, weed even helps

people lose weight, so it *must*
be good for you!!! Sure, the
munchies exist, but Ed would
never let me snack.

Yeah. Weed is
nice. Everyone
should have
some weed.
Okay, I am going
to sleep now.
Good night.

September 12, 2014

Self-control:
It's something I had so much of before.
It's something I lack entirely now.

I eat the size of a regular portion from the dish on the
stovetop before ever spooning any onto my plate. I don't
eat until I am full. I eat until I am on the verge of puking.

I will never eat this much again, I think to myself after
every meal. *I must regain my self-control.*

Yet, the very next day, I repeat the same mistake.

With junk food, self-control is not even an issue. But it
is with my three main meals – especially dinner – when I
overeat, worry, and hate myself even more.

September 19, 2014

I am such a fucking loser I will never make a volleyball team again my game has gone to hell I am a bundle of nerves on the court I cannot pass for shit I am too damn nervous and untalented honestly I will be really fucking lucky if I even make the first cut at any tryout why do I do this to myself tryout season stresses me out so much I literally had to go home from school today because I felt sick I was hyperventilating and crying in the washroom I could barely breathe I could barely eat what the fuck is happening to me maybe if I was actually good at a single fucking sport I would not have to worry like this every September fuck my life at this point I just want to quit volleyball too because I am the worst athlete ever I really just want to cry.

September 22, 2014

This morning I stared into the full-length mirror, and for the first time in what seemed like forever, I was not analyzing or pinching my body. It was my face I was focused on as I realized just how goddamn ugly I really am. My nostrils are too small, my plain brown eyes are boring, my sideburns are dark and growing, and, worst of all, my once-perfect complexion has now turned to shit.

I practically have craters on my fucking face; pimples the size of cherry tomatoes, scars from popping that resemble potholes in the goddamn road, and the redness of a fucking strawberry field.

Why am I suddenly breaking out like this? I even asked my mother for advice. Her reply literally caused steam to come out of my ears and my face to heat up like a kettle.

"You are eating too much fat, Danah," she said coolly. "Don't you realize how loaded your breakfasts are? Far too much nut butter and granola. Lay off it, all right?"

I can never fucking win with this woman, can I? First, I eat too little, and now, too much!? I don't think I've ever been so frustrated with her before.

I wanted to slug her in the face.

> *Why didn't you?*
> *Oh! I know why…*
> *Perhaps because she is RIGHT, you idiot.*
> *Fatty foods cause pimples just like they cause muffin tops.*

No. I won't forfeit my marvelous, massive breakfasts. They are the reason I even get out of bed in the mornings.

> *Breakfast and the fact that you*
> *have to work out, you lazy pig.*

Okay, fine, that too. Nevertheless, I refuse to be taken down by my own damn mother, who, at this point, seems to have completely taken Ed's side, leaving me alone and helpless as I desperately try to find an escape.

Who would have thought that it would be Mom who would drag me, kicking and screaming, back into the hole?

October 3, 2014

Normally, you will rarely find me procrastinating about schoolwork, but recently, I have been using the kitchen, the Internet, and the gym as reasons to be away from the books. So far this school year, I have really not been impressed with myself. My grades are still outstanding, but my work ethic and new studying patterns are a worry; I can't keep finishing up assignments and notes at 1:00 or 2:00 a.m. all week when I *should* have done them earlier instead of working out, eating, preparing food, or searching through vegan health blogs.

I really hope I can turn this school year around before these bad habits stick. After all, everyone says that grade 11 is when marks truly begin to matter, and while making top grades has never been a big issue for me, I need to ensure that everything goes my way this year so that I can be considered for early acceptance.

Whoa.

Am I really discussing *university* right now – something that seems so far off? Well, maybe it is a good idea, because the last thing I want is for the school year to completely pass me by, leaving me clueless about exactly what I want to study or exactly where I want to go.

I was planning on staying in the city to study because it's easier financially, and there is less of a transition to make. But what school is my top choice and what program I am interested in? I have no idea.

Social sciences and humanities have always been my greatest interests, so naturally, I have been considering law for years now. But after conducting some recent research, I realize that there are so many other options for me. I could go into journalism, politics, therapy, social work, education, international development. The possibilities are endless. All I have to do is rediscover the impressive discipline and work ethic I once had.

October 10, 2014

I hate it when I hear people talking about fitness and health food like fuck off none of you know anything you are all idiots that is my turf anyway seriously get the fuck out.

October 15, 2014

The scale at the gym stood staring me in the face…. It was so intriguing; so inviting; so harmless.

> *Step on it.*
> *Please, just do it.*
> *Now is the time; you must know.*
> *You have not weighed yourself in so long.*
> *Don't you want to make sure you haven't lost any weight?*
> *You see, even I can be harmless sometimes;*
> *I care about your health.*

My curiosity – and Ed's nagging – got the best of me as I strolled on over to the shiny, silver scale and took off my shoes. I raised my foot in the air to finally step on when suddenly, two young tweens in bikinis appeared at my side, clearly waiting to weigh themselves.

"Oh, uh, g-g-go ahead." I stammered.

I stepped aside and watched as the first girl read her weight.

"Aw man, I gained a pound!" she shrieked.

"What are you at now?" her friend asked.

"Never mind," the girl said, jumping off the scale. "I have to get down to 110, and I'm not there yet."

"I'm way fatter thank you. I'm at 126. God, why did I get the *worst* body?"

I couldn't stand to hear another word of this idiotic, triggering conversation. I ran out of the change room and I never looked back once, even as Ed called for me to return.

Are you fucking kidding me, Danah?
Are you going to let some silly little girls
scare you from weighing yourself again?
GET YOUR ASS BACK HERE, YOU WIMP.

I couldn't. I was too scared. It was so alarming to see such young girls – neither of whom could be over the age of twelve – obsess about their weight.

I wanted to say something, I really did, but what could I say?

"Oh, hey. You know, you really shouldn't think like that. You might develop an eating disorder just like mine! It is really not much fun, so yeah. Please stop and just enjoy eating while you're young, okay? Okay. Have a good day."

The curiosity regarding my weight is still eating me alive, but after watching a stupid, electronic box cause such anxiety, I knew that I must try my absolute best to avoid weighing myself for a long, long while…until recovery, I guess.

By the way, when is that coming? I have been waiting patiently for what feels like a decade. When will I get my reward, my trophy, my prize?

WILL

I

EVER?

October 17, 2014

I absolutely detest throwing away even the smallest bit of food. Nothing burns me up more than watching my sister eat a single bite before throwing the remainder of her dinner into the trash, or worse still, leaving it out to spoil. She does this constantly, even though she is well aware of how infuriating it is. I am lucky to be well-off in a blessed country, where I am always confident that I will come home to find food in the fridge. We all know that *many* others don't share the same good fortune…. And yet, we don't care.

"What does it matter if I waste a bit every now and then…?" my sister scoffs. "You are not the damn food police, Danah."

"It is the principle of the thing. Just don't put so much on your plate. It's as simple as that. Imagine how grateful a starving child would be for a fraction of the portion that is now – and will forever be – in the trash."

I am not trying to "save the world" by any means, or be the "damn food police," but it just isn't fair. It is not fair to the individual who cooked the food, nor is it fair to the individuals who would do *anything* just to have a bite of it.

OctobeR 31, 2014

Ed struck again on this dreary Halloween, as all of my friends went home from school to indulge in candy and cake, while I created some bogus excuse as to why I wouldn't be able to meet up with them until later in the evening.

Why haven't I left yet? Well, I had to walk very quickly from home to be at the gym for 3:45–5:00, then return home and do yoga from 5:20–5:50, then eat dinner from 5:50–6:00 because chances are they were all eating gross pepperoni pizza by this time, like a bunch of barbarians. Finally, I had to shower, get ready, and rant in my journal, which I am currently doing.

It isn't a huge deal that I'm missing a couple of hours of watching horror movies and eating junk food, but sometimes I really do wish that Ed would *not* always be the reason I arrive late for, or completely miss, outings with my friends.

Anyway, I should probably head off now before they get too curious about where I am.

November 4, 2014

I have been thinking that maybe if I were to go away for
university in two years, it would be far easier to adopt
a vegan lifestyle. After all, I wouldn't have my parents
constantly breathing down my neck and watching my
every move and my every meal. Then again, I wouldn't
have their money or support, either.

Wait one second…. Would I really allow Ed to affect my
crucial decision about what university I should choose?

This is *not* by any means a long-term relationship, Ed. If
you think you are planning on following me to university,
think again.

> *And if you think that you*
> *are getting rid of me any time soon,*
> *YOU think again.*

November 6, 2014

I don't understand why sometimes, I absolutely regret
eating fat-free meals especially on days when I work out
more than usual or when my growling stomach indicates
that I should have eaten more. Then on other days, I
scold myself for *not* having eaten fat-free. Take today, for
example. Just five minutes ago, I was convinced that what
I ate was fine for the day, and that it wouldn't change my
weight or health or body. But now, Ed has forced me to
think otherwise.

Yeah, maybe because you have just spent
the past few minutes gobbling bowls of
sticky rice and eight pieces of salmon sashimi.
What is wrong with you?
Have you no control?

Fuck. Is Ed right?

Am I ever wrong?

Why didn't I just eat a fat-free breakfast and lunch today
when I knew that I would have to eat out tonight for
dinner? I can feel every single piece of fatty fish and every
damn grain of buttery rice sitting in my stomach, and I
feel sick and anxious and disappointed and scared.

None of this would matter if I'd eaten fruit and a salad,
instead of fucking peanut-butter baked oatmeal for
breakfast and pasta for lunch. Why did I put myself
in this situation? Now, I have to go home and do my
emergency workout of 500 total reps of neck tugs, push-
ups, sit-ups, squats, and calf raises.

Don't forget you still have yoga practice to do.

Fuck my life.

November 13, 2014

I am out of control again.
The proof?
The rush of tears angrily pouring from my eyes;
the temper tantrum that just occurred
downstairs in the kitchen; the stomping of feet
and unnecessary slamming
of doors.

> But I don't care.
> I do not give a fuck.
> All I wanted to do was eat an
> early dinner but my mom is
> making me wait.
> What the fuck for?

Fuck you, Mom!

I want to eat the leftovers because I AM FUCKING
HUNGRY.

I spent all night and day with Grandma so why the fuck
must I wait for her NOW?

She won't mind!

> And even if she does, I do not fucking care
> because I AM HUNGRY AND I WANT TO
> EAT NOW!

I ate an early lunch, and I
have been looking forward to
these leftovers all day.

Now I can't eat for another
fucking hour.

And no, Mom, I will not just
have a snack, so fuck you.

And fuck you because I do
not want to walk the dog
with you right now.

Stop playing nice just because
you acted like a bitch.

November 13, 2014

I am disgusted by my words and actions earlier this
evening....

Ed,
What
Are
You
Doing
To
Me?

I am only doing what is best, baby.

November 19, 2014

Recently, I have become *obsessed* with the notion of volunteering abroad in India or Thailand. While doing volunteer work in developing countries has been a dream of mine for a couple of years now, I think that the real reason I have chosen these two destinations may be my passion for reading the blogs of famous vegans who eat delicious, healthy food and partake in spiritual yoga classes there.

Nevertheless, my desire to participate in one of these volunteer trips is growing stronger by the day. I spend hours online researching the dates, costs, and benefits of each potential trip. I plan to speak to Mother about it, but first I have to be extremely well-prepared if I am to convince this stubborn, cheap woman to allow me such a life-changing journey.

November 27, 2014

I am so sneaky and so very smart. Every night upon returning home from practice, I notice my parents eyeing me as I scan the fridge and cupboard; they want to see me snack. *Fine,* I think to myself, *I will snack.*

But that is a big fat lie.

I reach into the cupboard for a granola bar and do my best to look as though I intend to eat it. I stroll up to my room and even crinkle the wrapper a couple of times to make them think I'm opening it. Next, with a sinister smile on my face, I tuck it away – along with many other pieces of hidden food – in my bedroom closet.

Maybe one day, I really will snack after practice – you know, to refuel and all – but realistically, my practices aren't nearly intense and physically demanding enough to require refueling. Besides, I am normally still full from my huge dinner, I swear!

I'm afraid that someone will discover my secret stash of granola bars and food, just as someone is bound to discover just how fucked up and wicked I truly am.

Yes, you are wicked and sneaky and so very smart.
I could not be more proud of you right now.

December 1, 2014

I am so fucking tired of chasing the same oblivious, absentminded, handsome, kind, intelligent, humorous, athletic guy that I have been after for almost two whole years now. When will I realize that he does not want me?

> *When will you realize that no one ever will?*
> *There is far too much wrong with you.*
> *I mean, just LOOK at yourself.*

Ed is right, on this one. No one will ever want a girl like me. The second I even *think* I have the guy interested, I pull back as quickly as possible. My fear and insecurities stand in the way of ever developing *anything* remotely serious. I am a tease. I am a chicken. I ask myself, what there is to be afraid of. Sure, if I had a bit more experience in this department, there wouldn't be an issue. But the reality is that the longer it takes to get this experience, the farther behind I become, and the more afraid I am.

December 7, 2014

For the past month or so, I have been attending writing classes taught by a professional author at my local library. Since I aspire to be an author, this opportunity couldn't be any more exciting. But when the class was instructed to write and polish a piece by the end of the course, I really didn't know what I could offer.... Until, that is, I rediscovered my diaries from two years ago.

The words were painful to read and type – and yes, they were even triggering – but I knew that it was the only work I could show, because it's truthfully my best work. It is real. It is raw. It is frightening.

The class seems to agree, but more importantly, the teacher agrees. She sees "potential" in me, and hearing this is something I could never have dreamed of. She even offered to take me under her wing and asked if I would consider having my diaries published. I know this is a once-in-a-lifetime opportunity, but am I ready for the exposure if it really happens? Would I hide behind a pseudonym, or would I come out to the world about my struggles? I can only imagine how embarrassing it would be for my friends and family to discover exactly what goes on in this screwed up brain of mine, but I can also imagine how many struggling youths like me that I might be able to help. If they could find similarities between their current state and mine, then perhaps they would seek help before it's too late.

Oh, you want to go save the world now, eh?
Give me a fucking break.

But isn't that what writing is all about, helping and inspiring others? I really do think I have an incredible shot to finally *do* something with my life…. Will my selfishness and fears stand in the way? Do I lay everything out on the table for anyone and everyone to read?

December 10, 2014

I am so fucking
STRONG and HAPPY
and PROUD right now.
I just held plank for
eight minutes straight.

Next step?
Shoot for ten minutes.

I will reach that goal.
And I will not give Ed the credit.

December 12, 2014

I do not think anyone will ever understand the amount of planning that goes into my food and exercise routine every week. Although I no longer write down exactly what I am going to consume on a regular basis, I create a mental list so that everything comes together. I have to stay alert and flexible. If plans change, I must compensate.

If I eat too much or exercise too little on any given day, I adjust my requirements to fit. The process is both stimulating and exhausting.

Certainly, I am aware that this is not normal for most people, but it's normal for *me*. Frankly, I am happy living this way. And no one can tell me otherwise.

> *I completely agree.*
> *Looks like we are finally seeing eye-to-eye.*

December 18, 2014

My school volleyball season has finally begun, and while I am grateful for the additional practice to help me improve on my club team—

> *And while I am grateful for the additional exercise to help improve your physique...*

...I am also extremely nervous to represent my school and play in front of my fellow students. I know I definitely should not be nervous, since I am one of only three teammates with club experience. But I think that is part of the problem; I constantly expect far too much of myself, thus stressing out and playing like horseshit. It is evident that I am the weakest of the three club players too. I suck at sports, so I really do have to step it up and impress my peers and satisfy myself every time I set foot on that court. I admit that I have made some big improvements in my game, but my defense is the issue.

My placement and form are often perfect, yet the ball goes flying. You see? This is why I should quit sports.

December 23, 2014

"What are you writing?" Dad asks, as he enters my bedroom. I quickly shut my notebook and tuck it under the covers, but just as quickly I regret it. I have only sharpened his curiosity about just what it is I am writing.

"I'm working on a manuscript for my writing course," I reply, silently praying that he doesn't poke and prod for details.

"Wow, a manuscript! What's it about?"

Fuck. Seriously?

"I, uh, don't really like to talk about my writing…. I guess I'm shy, but you can read it later on, if you like."

"Sure, I would love to," he says, giving me a suspicious look and turning to leave.

Fuck.
He knows.
How could he not know?

Now he is going to go tell Mom that I am writing about my disorder and they will think I am sick again and they will be even more distrustful of me.

Fuck.
I fucked up.
What have I done?

December 24, 2014

The mirror's truth slapped me in the face this morning, as
I stared at my ass. I braced myself for the personal attack,
as my self-esteem took a plunge.

It is so saggy.
Why is it not firmer?
But I work out all the time!
Will it ever be plump and desirable?
I could have sworn it was not like this yesterday...
No one will ever want me when I look like this.
Since when am I embarrassed by my body?
I thought I was attractive and fit.
Is Ed controlling my thoughts again?

You know it, baby.

December 25, 2014

To save myself from the agony and punishment that
would have followed, I did not eat a slice of cake today at
Christmas dinner. This time, I ignored the eye rolls and
the disappointed expression on Mother's face.

Smart choice.

December 31, 2014

Alcohol is a dirty, dirty bitch. I can't stand to feel so out of control, just as I can't stand the thought of every single dirty calorie sliding down my throat with every shot. It is no secret that hard vodka and sugary coolers are loaded, but the social pressure to drink and to party manages to suppress the knowledge. I must fit in, after all. I cannot hide in my goddamn hole forever.

That's what you think.

January 2, 2015

Everyone knows that the New Year brings resolutions. I am prepared for the bullshit goals that follow – mostly from my mother and sister – about "losing weight" and "eating better" and "exercising more." Yes, the beginning of the year is especially hard on me, as everyone plays right into social media's trap. It's only two days into 2015, and I have already seen countless commercials for weight-loss products.

When you think about it, the messages and conflicting headlines in magazines are quite comical.

"Lose Thirty Pounds in
Just Three Weeks!"
"Learn to Love Yourself
and Your Body!"
"The Ultimate Best
Chocolate Cake Recipe!"

"My Eating Disorder Story Revealed!"
"Fitness Secrets From a Movie Star!"
"My Weight Gain Explanation!"

Am I the only one who can see how ridiculous this is?

I, for one, am making it my personal goal to balance *all* the aspects of my life, focusing on the delicate dance between my food and exercise, of course. Am I trying to

lose weight? Absolutely not. Am I trying to gain it? No.
I must find the power to maintain, and I must have the
confidence to indulge, or take a rest day now and then
without believing it will have a disastrous effect on my
weight and health.

Rest day?
Indulgence?
That's what you think.
A new year means a new you!
Time to lose a few pounds again.

Yes, I hear Ed loud and clear in the back of my mind, but
his words mean nothing to me today. I am confident that
my system will continue to work well for my body: three
large, yet "clean" meals, paired with an hour of personal
workouts and a half-hour of yoga daily. I eat a lot, so I
exercise a lot.

THIS IS BALANCE.
I KNOW IT.

Jesus, I do not think I ever want to hear the word *balance*
again. It is always on my mind, running ahead of me in
this grueling race; impossible to catch up to and attain.

Why is it so difficult to attain? There is no black or white
answer. I can only listen to my body, and – if Ed's voice
eases off – listen to my thoughts. This is what I struggle
with the most. I never *listen*. Perhaps *that* should be my
New Year's resolution.

January 5, 2015

Just two stores ago, I tried on this other beautiful form-fitting dress that made me smile from ear to ear; I looked lean and mature and elegant. It accentuated my curves perfectly.

This current dress, however, does the complete opposite. Somehow, it manages to place a flashing red light directly over my flabby lower belly, practically inviting everyone to stare at it.

I am horrified.

"Danah, are you coming out or what?" Mother calls.

I call back in a shaky voice, still upset by my reflection. "Uh…no, I don't like it on me."

"So, should we go back to that other store and buy the dress you liked?" Mother asks.

> *Do not even fucking bother.*
> *That will only expose your fat, too.*

"No thanks," I reply. That dress probably looked far more atrocious on me than I thought.

January 9, 2015

Panic and guilt and panic and guilt and panic and guilt
and panic and guilt and panic and guilt and panic and
guilt and panic and guilt and panic and guilt and panic
and guilt so I binge and purge and binge and purge and
binge and purge and binge and purge and binge and
purge and binge and purge and binge and purge and
binge and purge and binge and purge and binge and
purge again and again and again and again and again and
again and again until I hate myself more and more and
more and more and more every damn day.

Okay, so I may not have been doing the traditional form
of purging by sticking my finger down my throat, but I
have to admit that I was purging through over-exercising.

As I devoured a large stack of pumpkin pancakes with
maple syrup at a breakfast restaurant this morning, I
thought that I would surely gain weight. So naturally, this
caused me to skip lunch and spend the afternoon in the
gym and on my yoga mat. I was feeling good about my
decisions at that point, until the moment I arrived home
and realized how truly *famished* I was. So naturally, this
caused me to eat an entire box of pasta, ten miniature
cucumbers, and a few pieces of leftover chicken kabob.

Who the fuck eats that much in one sitting?

I felt terrible; I could barely stand; I could barely breathe.
All I could do was lie down and surrender myself to Ed
as he screamed and demanded that I get off of my lazy ass
and work off the thousands of calories that the monster
within me had inhaled. Naturally, this caused me to go on
an hour-long walk on the treadmill, and secretly do my
emergency workout of 1000 reps of neck tugs, push-ups,
crunches, squats, and calf raises like a fucking maniac.

"Danah, how many times have you done this now?"
Mother questioned me once I had finished complaining
about how sick and bloated I felt. "Learn from your
mistakes...seriously."

She was clearly irritated, but honestly, she had every right
to be. I have made this same mistake many times just in
the past month alone, and if I am growing tired of living
it, surely Mom is tired of hearing my complaining, the
heavy thumping of my feet on the treadmill, and the
constant sound of food being prepared in the kitchen late
at night.

This whole day just leads me to believe that I have really
made very little improvement over the past three fucking
years.

Maybe I
should just
never eat
or exercise
again and
just die….
That would
solve all of
my problems
now,
wouldn't it?

January 12, 2015

Carbs used to be my absolute enemy back in the midst
of my disorder a few years ago. It is so refreshing and
eccentric to see how far I have come and how far my diet
and lifestyle has evolved since then. Carbs are an absolute
staple in my diet now, whether they include complex
carbs like fruits and vegetables, or starches like pasta and
rice and potatoes.

I have been inspired by the vegan blogs on Tumblr and
Instagram, but also, it really has come down to preference.
I would much prefer a simple and very large bowl of plain
pasta with vegetables and chickpeas to a stew of meat or a
seafood dish. I am so envious of the glorious HCLF (high
carb, low fat) plates of food that I see from these vegan
stars online: so many *carbs* and so little *guilt.*

But alas, my parents will *never* allow me to go vegan – especially coming out of a disordered past – but what I can do for now is prepare myself for my future and really try to eat vegan breakfasts and lunches.

Will it be difficult to do so? Absolutely not, because animal product alternatives are what my body craves.

> *But is it what you truly crave,*
> *or is it what I am persuading you to crave?*

January 13, 2015

Why am I constantly fatigued? I really do mean *constantly*. Perhaps it is because I wake up at 6 a.m. every morning. I get six to seven hours of rest every night. Is this enough? Studies have shown that eight is ideal for a student, but that is simply unrealistic for me. Upon returning home from volleyball at 10:30 p.m., I must complete my daily yoga for 30 minutes, shower, finish studying, and then finally hit the bed. How can anyone this preoccupied get *eight* whole hours of sleep?

Sometimes, even on weekends, I blame my lack of sleep on my lack of late-night eating. My growling stomach wakes me up at six instead of letting me sleep in. After all, the latest I eat is 4:00 in the afternoon, and I never snack after volleyball or the gym in the evenings…. Normally water fills me up enough, but maybe this lifestyle is taking too much of a toll on my sleeping patterns.

Are you telling me that if you snack, you will sleep better?
What kind of a twisted world do you live in?
Get a grip; that way of thinking is absurd.
You will not snack late at night.
And you will not snack at all.
Stop being such a baby.
Nap if you need to.

But when I wake up after a nap, my mind assumes it's morning, so my stomach growls for breakfast. Napping just makes everything worse!

Okay, well then, suck it up.
I don't know what else to tell you.

January 16, 2015

I have this blurry memory of my friends feeding me a slice of bread when I was wasted as shit last night. If this is true, and I really was fed a fucking slice of toast at 2:00 a.m., I am going to flip.

How can I find out the truth? If I ask my friends, they will think I am insane and ungrateful for their help....

Their help?
Are you stupid?
Or should I be asking if they are stupid?
Everyone knows that feeding someone
carbs while they are drunk doesn't help.
They wanted to feed you late at night.

Your friends are terribly selfish.
They want you to gain weight.
Never again will you drink.

January 22, 2015

The school ski trip is just around the corner, and the déjà-vu of my anxiety regarding the grade 8 Quebec trip is terrifying. The questions are never-ending and always the same.

How will I work out?
What – and how much – will I eat?
How will alcohol affect my calorie intake?
Will my friends care – or even notice – if I restrict?
Will there be enough room and time for my daily yoga?
Is the plan to eat out at restaurants, or make our own meals?
Is Ed going to accompany me by hiding in my suitcase?

It worries me that I am still the anxious mess I was three years ago. But I have reason to be afraid. After all, four days and three nights really is a long time to dump the "clean" eating habits and intense workouts that I am accustomed to.

I want to talk about it with someone – a friend, preferably – but I know that I will only be judged, and pegged as the girl who has an eating disorder, just like I was on the Quebec trip.

Some things never change.

January 27, 2015

I scrape the sides of the food processor until the muscles of my arm plead for me to stop. I am so wired that I am unable to waste even the smallest remnants of food. I need the all of the nutrients and fats and sugars that I can get to compensate for the excessive exercise of the night before. While eating at only three points during the day, I make sure that I eat and lick until the plate is shining.

I wonder if this is normal.

I wonder if *I* am normal.

January 28, 2015

Daily Meals & Exercise Schedule 2015:

Day of the Week	Breakfast	Lunch	Work Out
Monday	Smoothie Bowl	Rice, corn, chickpeas	Chest & Shoulders
Tuesday	Baked Treat	Pasta salad	Volleyball Practice
Wednesday	Toast & Toppings	Couscous, lentils, veg	Tri, Bi, & Back
Thursday	Raw Treat	Pasta, tomatoes, tofu	Volleyball Practice
Friday	Layered Jar	Cauliflower rice bowl	Lower Body
Saturday	Yogurt Bowl	Pasta Salad	Home Workout
Sunday	Pancakes	Potatoes, roasted veg	Cardio

* EVERY LUNCH MUST HAVE A CARB, A FAT, & A VEGGIE

February 1, 2015

"Jesus, Danah, why do you always wear these gross, oversized sweatpants every time you leave the house?" Mother asked again this week.

I let out a hefty sigh. "For the hundredth time, Mom, I am just seeing my friends for a movie night. Everyone wears sweats. Can you please just get off my back?"

"No, I will not get off your back. Frankly, I am sick and tired of seeing my daughter hide her perfect figure in baggy clothes!"

I pushed past Mom to leave the house quickly, as my sister called out to me.

"And why don't you try a little thing called makeup every now and then? You look like you could be my brother!"

I do not care about clothes or makeup. And I don't see anything wrong with the way I dress. Sure, my clothes are often baggy when I go to school or a friend's place, but they are tight and sexy in the gym – just like my body. As for Mother suggesting that I hide my body, well, that is complete bullshit. I love my body; never would I want to hide it. These people think they know me. They don't know half of who I really am.

Yes, because I control that half of you.

February 4, 2015

Paranoia.

        Paranoia.

                Paranoia.

      Paranoia.

           Paranoia.

         Paranoia.

         Paranoia.

    Paranoia.

              Paranoia.

        Paranoia.

              Paranoia.

I constantly find ways to become paranoid and suspicious about practically everything related to my food.

What if, on their mission to have me gain weight, my family has been adding sugar and salt to my food all along? Or what if, after we've argued, my sister fucking *spits* in my food and touches all of it?

The idea terrifies me. It absolutely terrifies me. I should not be this afraid or paranoid, but I am.

I am.
I am.
I am.

I really am fucked up.

And it is all thanks to Ed

No need to thank me, baby.
Trust me, it is my pleasure.

FebRuaRy 6, 2015

Even after eating a whopping portion of pasta with loads
of beans and veggies, I am still able to fall in love with my
strong, sexy reflection in the mirrors at the gym.

Yes, sweat it out.
You are beautiful.

I can't disagree with Ed on this one; I really am beautiful,
especially when I sweat. Of course, I do have the
occasional complaint, but in general, I am so proud of
how far I have come in terms of my mental health. The
physical improvements are obvious, but this new level
of self-love and confidence for my figure and fitness is
indescribable. I am literally beaming. When was the last
time I smiled this brightly?

I have come to realize it is perfectly fine to be a little
screwed up at times. Everyone has a little demon poking

out every now and then. What matters is asking for help when it's needed and feeling radiant and proud when it's deserved. I am not perfect by any means – nor will I ever be – but I have grown to accept myself. I am surrounded by positivity and light.

I am an ambassador for self-acceptance and self-love; it is my duty to direct my friends on the right path when they go off on their rants:

> "I am the ugly one in our group."
> "Why can't my legs look like *hers!?*"
> "Jeans look so terrible on me."
> "There is no way I have the body to pull *that* off."
> "I really should eat less crap and hit the gym."

To that, I say *NO MORE*. Eat in abundance, and most importantly, eat whatever fuels you and whatever makes you joyful!

> *Who the fuck gave you a happy pill today?*

I don't know, Ed, but not even you can ruin my wonderful mood.

February 8, 2015

In a matter of two pitiful days, I have done a complete
180 about feeling body-confident and mentally healthy.
All of a sudden, I'm finding things right, left, and center
about myself that make me feel *nauseated*.

BUT
WAIT.
I
THOUGHT
I
WAS
HAPPY
WITH
MYSELF!

*Well, it looks as though you
are terribly, terribly wrong.*

February 9, 2015

The latest trend in the vegan community a 100-percent *raw* high carb, low fat diet. To be honest, I am not too certain if I even understand the point of consuming only raw food. Perhaps to better preserve all of the nutrients? And I don't know if I could ever adopt such a lifestyle. Trust me, I love fruits and vegetables just as much as the next vegan, but could I eat a massive plate of fruit for *dinner?* So much would have to eliminated from my diet if I were to go raw: baked oatmeal, cookies and granola bars…. Then again, they could all be replaced by raw dishes like soaked oats or frozen goodies.
Maybe raw is better after all.

It is, trust me.
Less cooking oil equals less fat.
More nutrients, fruits, and veggies
also *equal less fat.*
And what have we learned that
less fat is equal to?
Weight loss and perfect bodies.
And happiness, of course.
Yes, happiness.

February 20, 2015

Even though I am proud of myself – and extremely surprised – for *not* secretly exercising or practicing yoga during Mont Tremblant, I am disgusted about how ecstatic I was after puking up what must have been ten pounds of food (and alcohol) the very first night.

Does that make me bulimic? I honestly didn't do it on purpose, but the embarrassment of the night was soon erased by delight.

Yes! Now I am free not to exercise for the rest of the trip. I have practically no food left in me, I thought to myself the next morning after I had sobered up. *Even better, tonight, I won't have to eat OR drink, thanks to my hangover.*

I am sick.
I am so terribly sick.
Who even thinks like that?
I really thought I was recovering.
Now I realize there is no such thing as recovery.

February 23, 2015

I am so sick and tired of my entire family strolling into the kitchen while I cook, or appearing in the basement while I work out. Don't they see how fucking *obvious* they are? Do they think I am stupid?

No, they think you are still sick.
Ignore them. They only want to learn from you.
They watch you exercise because they want your toned body.
They watch you cook because they want your healthy diet.
Don't waste energy stressing over this.
Just take it as a compliment, baby.

But it's hard to take it as a compliment when it makes me feel like they still don't have a sliver of faith in me. It's funny how much time I've spent trying to escape the demon, when maybe it's my family I should escape from.

February 24, 2015

I have hit a yoga funk. The repetition of my daily practice has really been tough on me mentally and physically. My lower back is in constant pain, and deep down, I dread every time I step on the mat. But yoga isn't an option. I created a daily routine. I must perform it daily with the same level of competence in the same time frame. No exceptions. No changes. Besides, Ed will never let me back off now. I have no choice but to find my groove again – somehow.

I don't have the strength to support myself in the arm balances as long as I used to. I don't even have the flexibility I once had. Even worse, I don't have the passion to practice and to breathe like I used to.

And yet, you cannot stop.

February 28, 2015

Lately, I have been intrigued by the idea of getting a tattoo. I know, most teenage girls at one point dream of some sort of a stupid heart or infinity symbol on their wrist or hip. But the idea I have is far more meaningful and tender. After all, a tattoo is permanent—

As permanent as my presence—

so I must be comfortable with it for the remainder of my life. Although I fear it will inevitably remind me of Ed, I am hoping that it will remind me even more of how far I have come from this experience. I plan to have the beautiful recovery symbol from the dreaded 8th floor of the hospital tattooed behind my ear.

The design is simple, and yet, as I passed it every day on that glass wall before entering my usual room to step on that scale, it meant more to me than anyone could ever know. It is what got me through that summer. It is what I hope will get me through the rest of my life.

I was extremely reluctant to share this idea with anyone, for it is clearly very personal and secret to me. But then my sister approached me with her silly tattoo idea. I felt as though I had no other choice but to get it off of my chest and into the air around us. I needed to open up to someone…even if that someone was my selfish bitch of a sister.

I could feel the tension the moment I said it. She simply didn't know how to respond. I guess I can't blame her. If I was in that same scenario, I would be hesitant to respond as well. I think it was the simple fact that I *said* it in the first place that made all the difference. I think it means that I am beginning to get more comfortable with the idea of talking about my past.

Yes, it happened.
Yes, it was painful.
Yes, I will surpass it.

Yes, it happened.
Yes, it was delightful.
Yes, you will surrender.

March 3, 2015

"You really have not eaten much this entire weekend."

BLAH.

"Glad to see you finally eating, Danah!"

BLAH.

"Are you *sure* you wouldn't like any?"

BLAH.

"Promise me you already ate?"

BLAH.

Suddenly, I am transported back to my grade 8 self –
fatally skinny and mentally ill – as the soccer moms
questioned my eating habits. Certainly, I eat *far* more
than I did three years ago, but it scares me deeply to
experience this sort of questioning again. It makes me
question my ability to detect the demon's presence.
Maybe others have the power to do so even before I can.
Is it more obvious from afar? Or am I too sick to see
him sneaking up on me? Is he starting to awake from his
slumber; preparing for battle?

Oh, baby, I was never asleep.

I do not have the strength or the determination to
battle him again. Really, I don't. The fight has been far
too long and excruciating for me to handle. Normally,
I eat plentifully at tournaments, only this weekend,
it is difficult to convince myself to eat as much as my
teammates. They are playing and working it off, while I
sit on the bench for the entire fucking tournament. The
resemblance to my final soccer season is alarming. And
the worst part is that they expect me to eat *McDonald's!*
They are all insane.

And unhealthy.
Good for you, baby.
Do not be afraid to stick up for yourself.

I am grateful for their consideration, but I know what I am doing now; I do not need anyone's help anymore. After all, no one would know how to help me, anyway.

I AM THE ONLY HELP YOU NEED.

Yeah, yeah, whatever.

The irony of this entire situation really is quite comical. All I truly wanted in life – and essentially, what triggered my eating disorder in the first place – was to be a strong, impressive athlete. But as this weekend proved, I am the complete fucking opposite. I am a joke. I am terrible at all sports. I have zero talent. I have decided that that dream will be NO MORE. I am giving up on these fucking sports and the second this damn volleyball season ends, I plan to invest all my time and energy and passion in the weight room and the yoga mat.

March 4, 2015

I distinctly remember the expression on my sister's face when I told her how I plan to be vegan once I am out of the house.

"Are you *retarded?*" she snorted, ignoring my strong distaste for that word. "Veganism is practically killing you!" she continued.

"First of all, you don't know anything about a vegan diet or the nutrients humans need. Second of all, for someone who cares *so much* about the environment and the animals, you sure don't mind eating a good chunk of them. Being a vegetarian is pointless. Why choose to kill *some* animals and not others?"

"Why choose to kill *yourself* to be vegan?"

We argued on like this for hours, and those hours turned into days, and those days turned into weeks. For now, nearly every time she brings up how she "does not eat meat," I roll my eyes and scoff, and the ranting begins again.

Now, Saint Mother Theresa over here speaks non-stop about how badly she wants to go vegan, or about how badly she wants to save the environment, and frankly, I have had enough. She needs to stop stealing my thunder, my ideas, my lifestyle. Now I will look like the copycat, since she will surely leave home before me, and what is the first thing she will do?

"Be *retarded*" and go vegan.
Fucking hypocrite.

March 12, 2015

Even with all the weight training I have been doing – five times per week – I still look in the mirror and see the same, scrawny girl from two years ago.

Why am I not gaining muscle? It can't be that I am not

eating enough, because if that were the case, I really would not know what to turn to. Protein supplements, perhaps?

Never.
Those are far too loaded in chemicals and fat.

I want to be big.

Big?

Yes, big.

I want to resemble a personal trainer or a professional athlete.

I want people to look at me and automatically be intimidated.

Careful, darling…
Big muscle equals heavy weight.

Truthfully, it is the risk I am willing to take for this new desired look. Especially because, at this point, I still feel rather silly in the weight room compared to the beautiful, strong veterans. When will I come across as bold, tough, and knowledgeable like they do? Why am I not seeing real results in my strength and muscle tone?

March 19, 2015

"I really enjoy talking to one of my co-workers about nutrition because he is also very invested in a healthy lifestyle and gaining muscle," I said, excited to tell Mom all about the enriching and interesting conversations we have together. "He has a completely different philosophy. He weighs everything he eats and then inputs the information in this app to track his calories and—"

Mom didn't even let me finish the sentence before she interrupted me with a dark tone and an even darker threat. "Danah, I swear to God, if you *ever* do such a thing, I will send you right back to the hospital in a heartbeat."

What

'The

Fuck?

Where did this come from, and how had it escalated so quickly? She hadn't even given me a goddamn second to explain how much I disagree with his calorie counting. No. She automatically assumed that this would trigger my eating disorder. How pathetic, Mom.

Why does she not trust me, not even a little bit, not even at all?

I wouldn't trust you when you are with me, either.

March 26, 2015

I do not think I will ever be able to shake off this bizarre
habit of timing my meals. It makes me rush maniacally
– inhaling my food, not bothering to chew or to even
goddamn breathe – all so that I can finish my last meal
before 5:00 or 6:30 or whatever the fuck time it is. And
the end result is always the same: feeling sick to my
stomach and bloated for the remainder of the evening.

This is a habit I really want to kick because, quite frankly,
it's absurd to think that any major changes will occur if I
finish a meal five fucking minutes later. I mean, what is
the point of doing what I do?

> *Don't be stupid.*
> *The earlier you finish,*
> *the sooner you can work it off.*
> *You have to finish by the hour;*
> *this is not up for debate.*

Ed doesn't realize that after bingeing like this, I simply
don't have the energy to move until hours later. Whereas
if I had just taken my sweet time, eaten like a normal
person, and actually digested my food, then I would feel a
hundred times better than I do right now, with a massive
plate of undigested stir-fry causing my stomach to feel as
though it may burst.

I stood over the dish on the stovetop after sprinting home to make it by 4:50. I inhaled forkful after forkful until suddenly, too many noodles were in my system, blocking my airway. My heart hurt. I panicked. I was home alone with no one to save me if I really were to choke to death on the kitchen floor. Slowly, I told myself to relax, to breathe and to chew, and to breathe. Finally, the damn Chinese noodles went down.

Today's incident was really a wake-up call.

I have to draw the line somewhere. Ed, you are *not* going to kill me.

March 30, 2015

What should I whip up for breakfast?
    Healthified chocolate peanut butter brownies, perhaps?
        No, those are too high in fat, which I consumed a *lot* of yesterday....

Perhaps something lighter, like a layered chia seed pudding jar with yogurt and figs.
    Oh! Or maybe a smoothie bowl with all the fixings.
        No, we don't have enough bananas.

Fuck, how could Dad not buy enough?
    He should know by now that I eat at least two a day....
        God, how could he be so selfish?

Okay,

        Okay,

                Okay.

So how about pancakes with a caramel sauce of dates and cinnamon?

    No, I've been eating too much sugar lately, so perhaps dates aren't the best idea.

        Oh, but I adore dates *so* much.

Maybe I should read instead of spending this absurd amount of time in the kitchen.

    I have barely read a single page all summer.

        Maybe I shouldn't use the food processor at 6:00 a.m. on Saturday.

Whatever. They probably won't hear it anyway.

    Maybe I should quit obsessing about my breakfasts of the week.

        Actually, I don't care; I love planning ahead.

Maybe I should go ask the vegan idols what I should eat today.

    They give such amazing guidance whenever I am riddled with doubts.

        Positive, right…?

Most of them are haunted by disordered pasts, so they are a perfect source of advice.

    Maybe I should stop wasting time and do something productive.

No, wait. This *is* productive.

I am planning my future.
  Speaking of the future…
    what should I whip up for lunch?

March 31, 2015

Calm down.
                Calm down.
                                Calm down.
Just breathe.
                Just breathe.
                                Just breathe.
Fuck.
                Fuck.
                                Fuck.

FUCK. NO, OKAY, NO. I CAN'T JUST BREATHE. I
CAN'T. I CAN BARELY THINK. I FUCKING HATE
MY LIFE RIGHT NOW. ALL I WANTED TO DO
WAS PHOTOGRAPH MY FUCKING BREAKFAST
JAR, BUT MY FAT HANDS KNOCKED IT OVER,
SPILLING MY FUCKING HOMEMADE GRANOLA
– THAT LOOKED FUCKING DELICIOUS – ALL
OVER THE KITCHEN TABLE AND ONTO THE
FLOOR. WHILE I WAS SCREAMING AND CRYING
IN THE BATHROOM, MY SNEAKY MOTHER
TAKES THE OPPORTUNITY TO THROW IT
OUT. THROW IT OUT! INTO THE FUCKING
GARBAGE!!!!! IS SHE CRAZY???? SHE KNOWS

HOW MUCH I HATE WASTING FOOD. WHY
WOULD SHE DO THAT????? THE GRANOLA ON
THE KITCHEN TABLE WAS FINE. I FUCKING
HATE MY LIFE RIGHT NOW. I AM SCREAMING
AND CRYING ON MY BEDROOM FLOOR AND
PUNCHING AND THROWING ANYTHING IN
SIGHT BUT I DON'T CARE BECAUSE I FUCKING
HATE MY LIFE RIGHT NOW. I AM SO FUCKING
ANGRY. I HATE BEING THIS ANGRY BUT I
CANNOT CONTROL MYSELF, I REALLY CAN'T.
I STILL HAVE TO GO TO THE FUCKING GYM
TONIGHT BUT THERE IS NO WAY MY PARENTS
WILL LET ME AFTER THIS TEMPER TANTRUM.
I CANNOT EVEN FUCKING DEAL RIGHT NOW.
I WISH I COULD GO BACK IN TIME AND SAVE
THAT FUCKING GRANOLA AND SAVE MY FAMILY
FROM THE FUCKING MONSTER THAN I AM.

WHO AM I?

March 31, 2015

"Danah, you *must* learn to control your anger," Mother
tells me as she strokes my hair. "There are far more
important things in life to be angry about. There are far
greater problems than losing a bit of food." I know she is
right, but I cannot change my ways.

> *You don't need to change.*
> *There is absolutely nothing wrong*
> *with being passionate about food.*

Yes, passionate. That's all it is. Nevertheless, I am extremely grateful for – and surprised by – Mom's patience and support in the moments following my epic fit. I'm even more grateful that Father was still willing to drive me to the gym, even though I couldn't find the voice to ask.

April 1, 2015

Haiku to Ed

I crawl and clamber
But the darkness smothers me;
Rips away my soul.

April 2, 2015

Anxious and hesitant, I stepped into the majestic church. I was too busy stressing over the communion bread as opposed to appreciating His home – a place that I visit very infrequently. How can I be so selfish? Can Ed *please* stop nagging me at times like this? I told myself to just breathe, and to rely on God to give me strength.

Little did I know that just two minutes later we would be exiting the church before the mass had even begun. The overwhelming number of people and the limited available seating discouraged Mom from staying. A part of me felt extremely relieved, while another felt extremely ashamed. Not only had we missed Christmas mass this year, but now we were skipping Easter too! *I* was the one who persuaded Mom to attend mass today in the first place, but as we turned to leave, Ed wouldn't allow me to talk her into staying. I am sorry, God. Forgive me.

April 3, 2015

Dear my masterful Ed,

What crazy, sorrowful quests we have ventured on together! You have shown me what it means to truly be miserable and depressed. You have even shown me what it's like to contemplate suicide. You have encouraged me to absolutely detest myself, and you have even encouraged me to cry myself to sleep almost every night. For this, I thank you. You may think you have won, Ed, but I will never stop challenging you for my release and recovery. Please, Ed, spare us both all this trouble. Please Ed, set me free.

Your submissive, yet resistant

Danah

> *You can never escape.*
> *I am your disorder.*
> *I am your demon.*
> *I am YOU.*

✽✽✽✽✽

April 19, 2016

Oh, there you are, Ed. I haven't forgotten you are here.
It's just that I've been too busy living my life to talk.
It's strange how the tables have turned.
It seems I am in charge of you now!
I wonder where I should put you.

Did you expect me to wither up and die?
There is nowhere for me to be except in your mind;
And there is no place I would rather be, baby.
No person I would rather torment.

Don't worry.
I have accepted that you will stay indefinitely.
In fact, I have a proposition for you.

I'm listening.

If you agree to sit in the deepest, darkest corner of my being,
staying on your absolute best behavior
and speaking only when I summon you forward,
you can stay as long as you like.

You have that much power over me now?

I'd like to think so, Ed.

I'd like to believe that I'm a stronger person now,
physically and mentally; truly enjoying exercise,
as opposed to feeling obligated to do it.

I would like to believe that
I am a more compassionate person now,
embracing the beautiful vegan lifestyle for genuine reasons,
as opposed to striving for some impossible fantasy.

Oddly enough, Ed, I have you to thank for my new strength.
Without you, I wouldn't be able to
sense any trace of darkness approaching;
I wouldn't be able to stop myself from
returning to that deep pit.

Believe me, I have stumbled many times in the past year.
Staying strong and sane is very difficult at times.
But I have never completely fallen since we last met.
And never will I again.

Are you sure, baby?

Don't call me that…. I'm sure.
Now, go to the corner and sit down.
It may be quite a while before we talk again.

Whatever you say…Danah….

about the author

Danah Khalil was inspired to write at a very young age by
some of her favorite authors. This is her first novel, inspired by
her own life. She continues with her journal entries, fictional
novels, and poetry in hopes of inspiring others to tell their
stories through writing as well. Danah lives in Toronto.